CS THOMPSON

WHY KNOX?
REVENGE AT RHYTHM & ROOTS

A FIFTH NATASHA McMORALES MYSTERY

Published in the U.S. by:
James One Institute
Bristol, TN

Csthompsonbooks.com

ISBN: 978-0-9794116-9-4

BRISTOL AREA: WXBQ, Blackbird Bakery, Manna Bagel, Shooters Edge (Piney Flats), Machiavelli's, Benjamin Walls Gallery, KP Duty, Price's Store (Bluff City), George & Sids, Babycakes (Abingdon), Cottage Bakery (Kingsport), Chik-fil-a, Bristol BBQ

FLOYDFEST AREA: Hotel Roanoke, Blacksnake Meadery, Foggy Ridge, Natasha's Market Café, Nancy's Candy Company

WEAVERVILLE AREA: Stoney Knob Café, Well Bred Bakery, Salsa's (Asheville)

Acknowledgments

A special thanks to those who made significant editorial contributions (and corrections to my limited writing skill): Anne Southerland, Bob Land, Meredith Harbour, and Sarah Barker.

And for all sorts of other supports and advice: Alex Morris, Barb Thompson, Ben Walls, Cam Collins, Carol Rosenbeg, Dee Dee Galliher, Claire Hesser, Craig McDonald, Dyan Buck, Gary Rosenberg, Jenny Henley, and Leah Ross.

Also, for thirty people who let me "borrow" their names. Some of them I described as they are, some I took creative license with, and two I "killed." All gave their permission. A detailed list of names can be found in the appendix.

A special thanks to artist Kent Paulette, AKA Derfla, who let me use "The Dancer" for the front cover. Kent's work can be seen at www. DerflaPaintings.com.

Prologue

Baby Rose, she thought as if she was only now noticing the shade of lipstick she had just put on. At $32 a tube her Dior Baby Rose was the most expensive lipstick she used. Pouting her lips at the mirror she stepped back and surveyed herself. Her sandy blonde hair was gathered at the back of her head with a clip. The calico peasant skirt was loose enough to hide her least favorite feature, her hips, and the denim work shirt that flowed enough to hide her figure. She wore the shirt open, and under it her tight white camisole was doing its job. It was the clean-cut, country-girl-next-door version of dressing to kill. If she had been wearing her usual uniform there would have been no camisole, her shirt would have been buttoned near the top, and she would have worn a darker shade of pink. Maybe she would have worn Maybelline's Fifth Avenue Fuchsia or Revlon's Coralberry, her everyday lipsticks. Often she would wear no lipstick at all.

"What do you think you are doing?" she asked herself. This is how she dressed for Mark, not that it had ever done her any good. She knew she looked good. She had been told so many times by many men. "Men may watch women with alabaster skin and ruby red lips but because those women look like statues"—that is what the men told her. "Men don't want to hold those women," they would say. "Your lips look like candy," they told her, but she only heard that when she wore Baby Rose.

She smiled innocently, the way only a clean-cut country-girl-next-door could. She knew how to smile and she knew when.

Her head shook involuntarily as her sweet daydream drifted into something else. *If you know so much about prepping a hook this way, then why is it that only the wrong men take the bait?* Although she was alone in her bathroom, an angry look flashed across her face. Her eyes grew narrow and her chin rolled forward. It had been that way forever, and she was mad about it. Every guy she had ever wanted was her friend. Every guy she wanted to kiss told her how beautiful she was, and then kissed someone else. She had no idea what it was, but she knew—deep in her heart—that something about it all was just not fair.

She had not extended herself since high school like she was doing for Mark. That was many years ago. Since getting her master's degree in social work she had many opportunities with flirtatious men who could care less about her but wanted a taste of candy from a good girl. She could have had that anytime she wanted, but why would she want that?

She was not sure she could have what she wanted: a bad boy she could be bad with, but one who would be good with her when she wanted that, too. And then she discovered the morning show on radio station WXBQ. It did not take long for her to convince herself that Mark could be everything she wanted. She knew that if she could just manage to connect with him, he would know it, too. She wore Baby Rose lipstick and white camisoles for him, and he had noticed. She had seen him notice.

As a social worker she was generally out in her car, driving from one home or school to another, visiting her cases and attending meetings. The job was perfect in that it afforded her the freedom to make sure that every time Mark and Steve went on location for their show, she could place herself somewhere in Mark's line of sight. There was just one problem: Steve.

Steve was in the way. It was that simple. Mark was never going to make a move toward her if Steve kept doing it first. She told Steve no, she told him she wasn't interested in him, she threatened to tell the police and even threatened to tell his wife, but to no avail. Steve simply had to go. It was not her fault. She had done everything she could, but he would not take a hint.

Pulling some hair loose from the right side of her head she made sure that it did not match the few loose hairs on her left side. "It's no good to look like you're trying," she told herself as she turned out the light and left the bathroom.

Standing in front of her bureau she retrieved the envelope from her jewelry box and took out the money. Counting it again she confirmed twenty $100 bills. It was the money she owed him, and it would not do to be short. Putting the money in her bag she looked at herself again in the mirror over her bureau.

"You don't even know him," she told herself. It was true. She had only met him twice, once while he was still in jail and then again to give him the first $2,000 when he got out. He guaranteed to "fix" everything for "Four thousand bucks and a favor."

He had rugged good looks that most women would have liked but he knew it, and that was a turnoff to her. He was the baddest bad boy she had ever known, and in her line of work she had met many. But he would never have been good when she wanted him to be good. So, *Why am I wearing Baby Rose?* she wondered. Maybe it had something to do with how he flirted. It was not so much that he said the most vile and outrageous things to her. It was that when he said those things to her he never blinked. It was like he was completely confident that he could eventually charm her into anything he wanted, so he did not waste time or energy being clever or coy. "So why are you wearing Baby Rose?" she asked herself again as she left her bedroom.

"It's about time," she said as he strolled over to the picnic table he had chosen for a place to meet. "You're twenty minutes late." She was frustrated, and she wanted him to know it.

3

Through a crooked smile he calmly observed, "I love the way your mouth looks when you say the word 'you.'" Instead of sitting across from her, he came to her side of the table and stood over her, looking down.

She automatically held her palm against her camisole, but his eyes never strayed from her own. "I'm burning up," she said.

Glancing around, he spotted another picnic table under some trees. "Why didn't you just sit over there in the shade? You could have watched this table from there." Stepping back he held out his hand.

She looked at the other empty table. It was a bit embarrassing that she had not thought of that herself. So she was not angry anymore, but now she was embarrassed. *Why am I always so emotionally off-balance with this guy?* she thought.

Taking his hand she let him lead her to the other table.

As they walked he held her elbow tightly against his side. Leaning toward her, he asked in a whisper, "Do you have the rest of the money?"

"Yes," she said, pulling her head away from him. "Is it . . . ?"

"It's finished," he said, chuckling as he watched her struggle for the right word. "I'll show you a picture from my phone when we get settled over there."

They arrived at a lone picnic table near the wooded area. She took the bench facing Steele Creek Lake and was surprised when he circled the table to sit next to her.

"I just want to make sure nobody is watching us," he explained.

"Why would anybody be watching us? Nobody knows yet, do they?"

"No," he said with a wave of his right hand. "It just got done. That's why I was a little late."

"You went to his cabin, right?"

"Relax," he told her, rubbing her thigh with his left hand. "It went just the way you wanted it to go."

Removing his hand with her own, she demanded, "Show me the picture."

"Sure," he said, setting his phone on the table in front of them. "I've got it right here, but first I need more information."

"You want another favor?"

"Not another favor, darling. What I want is information about the first favor."

She stared at him.

"You know that boy who killed the state trooper?" he asked.

"Oddie Pruitt," she answered. "Of course I know him. At least I know who he is."

"Well, how did you know that he's the one that killed the cop?"

"His girlfriend—actually his ex-girlfriend—is a client of mine."

"Do you know anything else about him?"

"Like what?" she asked. The questions were confusing to her. She had given him information that he could use to plea bargain a suspended sentence. It was information that got him his freedom. It did not make sense for him to be second-guessing it now.

He tipped his head forward and looked at her like she was stupid. "I want to know if he has family or friends who are going to come looking for me."

With a shake of her head and a curl of her bottom lip she dismissed his concern. "Absolutely not. He's a rogue with no connections and no organization. I doubt even his mother cares."

His right arm disappeared around his side as he leaned toward her, studying her eyes intently.

"How about showing me that picture?" she said, trying to hide her discomfort as she placed the envelope containing the rest of the money on the table.

"Sure," he said, picking up his phone with both hands. "They were both there when I got there," he told her, maneuvering his touch screen with his finger.

5

Straining her neck to see the picture on his phone she asked, "Is that why it took you longer? Because you had to get rid of Mark first?"

"Yeah," he said in a tone that made her sick to her stomach. "I had to get rid of Mark first." With a sardonic grin he held the picture of Steve's living room out for her to see.

Gasping, then holding her breath, she lunged at the camera as if that would change what she was looking at. "You . . . killed . . . them . . . both!" she said with a look of horror and disbelief that did not change when the .38 slug tore through her forehead.

Had anyone been in the field to witness what happened, they would only have heard a whispered thump and then watched a country girl lay her head down on a picnic table and go to sleep.

Part 1

BRISTOL

CHAPTER 1

A Late-Night Visitor

"Don't move a muscle," said Nattie sternly as she leaned over him, clamping her left hand across his mouth. She let go of him when his eyes got big. As she stood up her right hand came around her body holding her Glock semiautomatic. In a single fluid movement, she pushed the weapon toward her left hand, holding the slide where she chambered a 9mm hollow-point bullet by shoving the handle forward with her right hand.

Nattie was all business at the moment, so she did not notice the degree to which Nathan was mesmerized watching her. The only gun he had ever seen her use was the Sig Sauer P238 he had chosen for her, thinking it was more suited for a woman. Her 9mm Glock was a much larger gun. He was entranced watching her handle it.

Holding the gun out in front of her she crept silently toward the kitchen, where the noise had come from. When she was halfway past her dining room table the kitchen light snapped on, which made her freeze for a moment before she continued. The kitchen light going on had a much more startling effect on Nathan as he found himself in a standing position holding his hands over his mouth.

He held his breath as she disappeared into the kitchen. The silence that ensued was broken by a crash that sounded like a Volkswagen driving though the pots and pans section of a Bed Bath & Beyond. It took a moment for him to finally come out of his trance. He rushed by the fireplace, grabbing a poker as he went. Holding the poker over his shoulder he followed Nattie into the kitchen.

He quickly surveyed the scene before him. Nattie's handgun was on the floor along with several pieces of cookware and the contents of the golf bag she kept by the back door. In the middle of the kitchen floor, standing six foot and change, was a youngish-looking black man with his arms wrapped around Nattie. Her arms were pinned to her side, and she was being held dangling a foot off the ground.

Nathan was sure that the man was squeezing her ferociously because if she could have gotten her lungs to work surely she would have been screaming. Had he been more skillful he would have realized that the element of surprise was on his side. Had he been trained he would have picked up the gun and put it in the kid's face before the kid knew he was there. Having neither skill nor training he held the poker up over his head and announced his presence with a scream.

The young man looked up and saw the poker come arching down toward his head. Instead of letting Nattie go and protecting himself with his arms he held on to her and spun around so that his back was toward Nathan. The staff of the poker crashed down across the back of the man's head, crumbling him to the floor.

"What are you doing, Nathan?" yelled Nattie from beneath her assailant.

Confused by Nattie's tone, Nathan held his tongue.

"Help him up, Nathan," she continued.

The kid had gotten his weight off of Nattie, but he remained wobbly on his hands and knees.

Squirming out from under him, Nattie reholstered her weapon. Kneeling next to him she asked, "Are you okay, Eli?"

"I think so," he said slowly.

Nattie remained in a squat next to him. Rubbing across his back she told him, "Take your time getting up. I'm going to get you an ice pack." Then, turning toward Nathan, she scowled, "This is Eli."

"I thought Eli was a kid," Nathan said, defending himself.

"He's fifteen."

Eli tried awkwardly to get to his feet. When he faltered both Nattie and Nathan took hold of his arms.

"I don't know what to say, Eli," offered Nathan. "When I heard the crash and walked in and saw you holding her . . . Well, you know what I thought. Sorry."

Two years earlier Eli was just a thirteen-year-old who, in an effort to avoid unpleasantness between his mother and her boyfriend, would wander through Bristol at night. After reading about Nattie's detective exploits in the *Bristol Herald Courier* and discovering that her back door was broken, he realized her home was an ideal refuge. At first he only stayed there when she was out all night on surveillance. He eventually got so comfortable on her couch that he sometimes slept there while she was upstairs in her bedroom. On one occasion she was on the couch herself when he broke in. She had been prepared to shoot him that night as well, but after talking to him she added him to the ever-growing group of men she mothered. The back door stayed broken, and he became a valued member of her collection for, in spite of his youth, he was an accomplished bakery chef. Whenever he enjoyed her hospitality he left some sort of baked goods behind.

Eli was hiding in the pantry closet the night Trace Noble attacked Nattie in her kitchen. He would have tried to protect her had Beau Robinette not been there to take care of it. Since Beau needed anonymity, Eli got the credit for the rescue. The *Bristol Herald Courier* touted him as a hero. He was faithful to Nattie to keep the secret.

For the last two years Eli had attended a boarding school outside of Roanoke, Virginia. His mother, a successful writer of cookbooks, had the resources to send him where he wanted, and he chose the Livingston Academy because of its culinary track.

"That's okay," Eli said, rubbing the back of his head. "I understand."

The two men shook hands.

"I'm Nathan."

Trying to smile, "I'm Eli."

"This is my ex-husband, Eli," said Nattie, resting a hand on Eli's arm.

Shifting into a typical fifteen-year-old's blank stare, Eli waited for further communication from Nathan.

"So, Eli, what brings you to Bristol?" asked Nathan.

Turning to Nattie, "I heard about what happened last week. I came to see if you were okay."

A look of confusion crossed Nattie's face, "Really? How did you hear about it?"

"My mom told me yesterday," answered Eli. "I was able to bum a ride tonight so I thought I'd come down and check on you." Looking around the kitchen he added, "I've got a new coconut muffin recipe I thought you'd like."

"I'm sure I will, thanks, but you didn't have to do that. I'm fine." She looked at each man knowing they did not believe her. "Look, guys, I admit that it is awful to have someone you care about die in your arms. I hope neither of you have to go through that. I mean that. But Marissa died well. She really did. She held on to her faith to the end. She's fine."

Nathan's head bucked back as she finished.

"What's wrong?" she asked him.

Nathan and Eli looked at each other.

"What is wrong, Nathan?" repeated Nattie.

"Do you know what you just said?" he asked.

After a quick glance at Eli, Nattie looked back at Nathan. "No, what did I say?"

"You said, '*She's* fine.' Not 'I'm fine,' but 'She's fine.'"

Nattie frowned as she shook her head slowly.

Eli just listened and watched.

Nathan grew restless. "Look, Nattie, this may not be the right time to say this, but it isn't about her."

His comment earned him another disapproving look.

"It's about you."

Her face softened. "You know, Nate, you're right. This isn't a good time for this. Eli and I have some catching up to do, so maybe it's a good time for you to head home."

Hearing his dismissal he grew morose. Taking Nattie by the elbow he ushered her to the dining room. "Excuse us a moment, Eli," he said over his shoulder.

Eli nodded and began picking up the golf clubs.

"Are you sure you're safe?" Nathan asked in a whisper when they reached the living room.

"No offense, Nathan, but the only time tonight I haven't been safe was when you tried to save me."

CHAPTER 2

Nattie (Two Weeks Later)

WHAT WAS THAT NOISE? NATTIE WONDERED, waking with a start. She lay very still on the couch in her living room while trying to discern the source of the noise. After a minute of silence she questioned if she had even heard a noise. Then she wondered what time it was and why she had been asleep on her couch instead of upstairs in her bed.

A slight attempt to move revealed stiffness in places she hadn't considered. She had been sleeping on her back. She never slept on her back, because when she did, she would sleep with her mouth open, and sooner or later the taste of her teeth would wake her up, as it did this time. She surrendered back into the couch in disgust and immediately felt her 9mm Glock, which was still holstered at the small of her back. Rolling forward she maneuvered into a sitting position and withdrew her gun, clip-on holster and all.

What was I thinking? She sat leaning forward, holding the gun and trying to reconstruct the circumstances that led her to that moment. Then the phone rang.

"Uhhhh, Sis," Kevin said cautiously into the phone. "Aren't you up yet?"

"Do I sound like I'm up?" said an irritated Nattie. "What time is it anyway?"

"It's ten o'clock."

Nattie turned toward the window behind her and immediately turned her face away from the sunlight coming through the window. "What do you want, Kevin?" she moaned into the phone.

"I was kind of wondering if you were coming in to work today."

" 'I was kind of wondering if you were coming in to work today,' " she repeated in a whiny voice, mocking him.

"Natalie Miriam," came the sharp voice of her mother, Ingrid. "You listen to me. This has gone on long enough, young lady. You get your fanny out of that bed and come down here to your office right now, or we're coming up there to get you."

Although she made no move to get up, or even stretch for that matter, Nattie was wide awake now. Thinking of nothing to say she said nothing.

"That's fine," Ingrid said after less than a minute of silence. "I'll be there at eleven to pick you up for lunch."

"That's okay, Mom," Nattie pleaded, hoping to sound somewhat gracious. "I appreciate the offer, but . . ."

"I wasn't offering anything, Nattie. I'm *telling* you to get up, brush your teeth, shower, and wash your hair. We'll be there at eleven."

"So," Nattie said smugly, "I don't have to get dressed?"

If Ingrid had been in the room she would have seen Nattie's head shimmy back and forth like a seventh-grade girl making a point. As it was, Ingrid did not even hear the comment, because she had already hung up.

Nattie began the laborious trip upstairs.

It had been almost a month since Marissa Ferguson had died in her arms. She had spent the first two weeks either telling people she was fine or explaining why she was not more torn up. She had even wondered if something was wrong with her, because she did not feel anything.

Then she started cutting things out of her life. She had not been to Blackbird Bakery in two weeks. She had not been to Manna Bagel in a week and a half. No yoga. No Shooters Edge. She told Debbie she was working, but she was not. She went out of her way to take jobs requiring all-night surveillance, which kept her out of the office. But for the last two days she hadn't left her house except for fast-food runs. It had never occurred to her that anyone might notice. Nattie lifted her head and looked at herself in the mirror over her chest of drawers, *I can't believe you called your mommy, Kevin,* she thought. Closing her eyes she exhaled slowly.

Nattie's ex-husband, Nathan, had been the only one with whom she had kept in contact. She had been with him the one and only time she had cried. He had held her with a tenderness she would not have known to solicit. Since then, the rule that she had made him agree to before all this happened—no physical contact and only one date a week—was rendered null and void. They had not agreed to drop the rule. They had not discussed it at all. And now he was once again a fixture in her life.

They had been together nearly every day since the night she had cried. Even for the past three days, when his presence was demanded at his tavern, he had called her on the phone several times a day. He could not have been sweeter. She could not have felt more out of control. She studied herself in the mirror again and chose not to think about Nathan.

She was surprised at how good it felt to let the warm water just rain down on her, considering the effort it was to get herself undressed and into the shower. Soap was more effort than she was willing to expend, but dirty hair would not escape her mother's inspection. Shampooing did not have the power to make her feel good, but it felt normal enough that she did not notice doing it a second time.

Wearing a thick terrycloth robe and toweling her hair dry she ambled into her bedroom with no idea of what she would wear.

"Mother!" she half screamed as she removed the towel from her face, discovering Ingrid standing in the middle of her bedroom, holding a blouse by the hanger in each of her hands.

"Which one?" asked Ingrid as she displayed a blue blouse and a green blouse.

"I don't care."

Laying the blue one on top of a pair of jeans she had already laid out on Nattie's bed she said, "This one then." The green one she returned to the closet. Without looking at Nattie, Ingrid headed toward the door, announcing, "I'll give you ten minutes to get dressed and come downstairs."

Nattie had not moved since being startled by her mother's presence. "Why ten minutes? You told me I had until eleven."

Stopping in the doorway she turned to face her daughter. "Things have changed. You're meeting a new client at eleven thirty. We'll get lunch after that."

"No, I'm not." Nattie's jaw pointed defiantly at her mother. "I've got all the cases I can handle right now."

Ingrid smiled at her daughter. "One more won't hurt."

"Kevin knows not to do that."

"I was there when the call came. I told him to make the appointment for you. You're going to want this one."

Nattie closed her eyes. It was all too much. She stood there silently until she felt her mother's hand on her cheek.

"Honey," Ingrid said softly. "Don't think. Just move. When you feel this way, you can't afford to stand still and think."

Nattie scrutinized her mother's face. It was showing age, but she could still turn the head of a high-school-age boy. "How would you know about that?"

"I've had my share of tough times, too, you know."

Pulling her robe tighter around her middle, Nattie replied, "I've never seen you have a bad day."

"You certainly have seen me have bad days. You just never saw me stand still. Don't you remember what we went through with your father?"

"Of course I remember what we went through, but none of that ever rattled you."

Ingrid's eyes narrowed slightly as she tilted her head. "Don't think for a moment that I wasn't rattled."

Forgetting that this was her mother before her, Nattie saw a woman who might have the kind of wisdom that comes from persevering.

"I know you think of me as a princess, Nattie, but remember I was raised by farmers. Like you, I'm tougher than I look." She returned to the door and added, "Besides, when your father left, I had to keep moving." She paused. "I had two kids."

CHAPTER 3

Knox's Mother, Roberta Farmer

"ARE YOU NATASHA MCMORALES?" The fiftyish woman lunged at her from the middle of the waiting room. Black stretch pants, a yellow knit top, and a floral jacket made her look like *Everybody Loves Raymond*'s Marie Barone from the neck down. She wore her dark hair in a flip, framing a face that could have passed for an aging Kate Beckinsale.

Nattie thought for a moment to explain once again who she is and why that name was on the door, but it was more effort than she wanted to expend. "Yes, I'm Natasha McMorales."

"We're Mel and Roberta Farmer." The woman introduced them both.

Mel, who had been standing behind his wife, looked like he would rather have been anywhere else. Dress slacks, a blue polo shirt, and a checked sport coat presented the stereotype of a used car salesman from the 1960s. A glance from Nattie in his direction brought Mel to life.

"Mel Farmer here," he said, waving a business card his hand. "Mel Farmer of Farmer's Fleet. Your next used car is already in our fleet."

Nattie took the card and immediately repressed a smile and the thought that he was the stereotype come to life. "Thank you. Now, what can I do for you?"

Roberta made a face at her husband, nudging her head in Nattie's direction. It looked to Nattie like Roberta wanted Mel to answer her question.

Mel stepped back.

"It's about our daughter," Roberta said. "She needs protection."

"'Protection,'" repeated Nattie. "That's not exactly our line. We are more of an investigation agency. I'm sure I can recommend someone who will be more in line with what you are looking for."

"We're looking for you, Ms. McMorales. We want you to find out who is stalking her."

"A stalker. I see," said Nattie. "Let's continue this in my office, shall we?"

Kevin gave Nattie a toothy grin and a thumbs-up as the Farmers walked past him into Nattie's office.

"Grab a pen," she told him, "and join us."

Kevin had never been asked to sit in on an initial consultation. For Kevin it was something new to experience. "Cool," he mumbled in a low voice as he looked for a pad and pen

"Do you know our daughter?" asked Roberta. She and Mel were seated in the upholstered chairs facing Nattie's desk.

Nattie was still settling into the chair behind her desk as she realized that there was an expectation that she should know their daughter. After a quick survey of her memory Nattie said, "I don't recall a Farmer. Does she know me?"

"She's in show business," said Roberta. "She goes by Knox—"

"Knox DeVilla," blurted Kevin, who after seeing there was no chair for him had gone back for his desk chair. He was just wheeling his chair alongside Nattie's desk when he recognized the name.

"You know Knox," observed Roberta.

"Oh yeah," answered Kevin. "I don't 'know her' know her, but I've seen her and the UTs around town a few times. O'Mannon's and Our House." He turned to Nattie, "She sounds a lot like Alison Krause."

19

"That's what everyone who hears her says," beamed Roberta.

"Knox DeVilla and the UTs," mused Nattie.

"That's her stage name. Isn't it clever? Candace is her real name. We used to call her Candy. It was her idea," bragged Roberta.

"Ummm," Mel intoned and then cleared his throat. Waiting until Roberta turned to face him, he then said, "Honey, why don't you explain to Natasha here why we came?"

"That would be good," agreed Nattie.

Roberta opened her giant handbag and took out an envelope. Handing it across the desk, she stated, "This came in the mail yesterday."

Nattie examined the plain white business envelope. It was a self-adhesive envelope, so there would be no saliva for a DNA test. The postmark was from Bristol, Tennessee, the day before it was delivered. The address was computer generated on a stick-on label, and the envelope showed no return address.

Inside the envelope was a single sheet of paper folded in threes. The computer-generated Old English font simply said "KNOX" at the top, followed by photos of two men. Underneath the two photos the letter read, "YOU'RE NEXT: SEE YOU ON STAGE."

Kevin, standing over Nattie's right shoulder, studied the photos along with her. "Who are those guys?"

"Do you remember a story in the paper about six weeks ago? A couple of WXBQ disc jockeys were murdered."

"That's Mark and Steve," Kevin pointed at the pictures. "I listened to them all the time, but I never knew what they looked like. They did the morning show."

"What happened to them?" asked Nattie.

"They were—" started Kevin before realizing Roberta had also begun to speak. After receiving a go-ahead tip of her head, Kevin continued, "They were assassinated at Steve's cabin. That's the word the *Bristol Herald Courier* used. They were found sitting next to each other on the couch with 9mm bullet holes in their foreheads. There was no sign of forced entry or theft. There are no suspects."

"Do you mean someone just walked into that room and fired two shots?" Nattie asked.

"What kind of person does that?" asked Roberta.

"Someone with absolutely no conscience at all," answered Nattie. "Is there a connection between your daughter and these guys?"

"No, not that we know of," answered Roberta.

Mel nodded his agreement.

"She didn't know either of them personally?" asked Nattie.

"No."

"Did she ever perform where they were, or did she ever try to get one of her recordings on their show?"

"No, nothing."

"Maybe I should be talking to your daughter now."

Roberta scooted forward to the edge of her chair. "I can assure you that my daughter cannot tell you anything that I can't tell you."

Nattie studied Roberta's face. Clearly she believed what she had just said. "I still think I'm going to need to talk to Knox."

Roberta turned her head slowly toward Mel, who promptly cleared his throat again. "I don't think that's a very good idea."

"Why is that, Mr. Farmer?" asked Kevin.

"Our daughter has emotional problems. If she knew about this, it would be very upsetting to her."

Leaning against the edge of her desk, Nattie explained, "Your daughter is being threatened. It should be upsetting to her. At the very least she needs to be warned, and she may have something to offer in an effort to protect herself."

"I, ahhh, think you'll find that your investigation will go much smoother without our daughter's help," Mel reiterated.

"Mel is right. Knox is high strung."

"She's a drama queen is what she is," added Mel.

"I assure you, Ms. McMorales, everything will go much easier if we leave Knox in the dark."

Nattie and Kevin exchanged a knowing glance that, when they were younger, meant, "Are you hearing what I'm hearing?"

"Do you mind if I am perfectly straight with you?" asked Nattie.

"Straight is what we want, Natasha. We are nothing if we aren't straight shooters," declared Roberta.

You don't have a clue what straight shooting is, thought Nattie. "I don't have the staff to set up protection for your daughter on a twenty-four-hour basis. I'm sorry, but it is the truth. If you want to hire us as investigators, we would do our best to find out who sent this note, but hear me when I say this: If you hire me I will do what I think is necessary to protect her."

"Excuse me, young lady," Mel said without clearing his voice first, "I thought you said you would not let us hire you to protect her."

"What I said was that I cannot accept the job of giving her twenty-four-hour protection. If I am hired to do the investigation, the goal of that investigation will be her safety. If it was my daughter I'd want to hire an investigator to find out who we're dealing with *before* they attempt anything."

"That is what we want," declared Roberta.

"I'm glad to hear that," said Nattie, "because if I ever think it's in Candy's best interest for her to know what's she's facing, then I will tell her."

The Farmers looked at each other.

Kevin looked at his sister as if she were speaking Martian. "I think what Natasha means is that if you hire us, we will place the highest premium on keeping Knox safe. That will be our most important thing."

"I am confident that once you get to know Knox, you will agree with us that she will need to be kept out of the loop. Don't you agree, Mel?"

Mel nodded affirmatively.

Way to take a position, Mel, thought Nattie, fighting the temptation to roll her eyes.

"Your agent here," Roberta said, gesturing toward Kevin, "has already explained your compensation, and we are ready to hire you. Aren't we, Mel?"

No one looked to see if Mel nodded, although Nattie did look at Kevin after being referred to as her agent.

"We will agree to your conditions, but first," continued Roberta, "we need you to agree to ours."

"Okay, let's hear your conditions."

"Well, right now we don't feel the need for twenty-four-hour protection. Besides trying to find out who sent that note, we want you to travel with us when we go to her engagements."

"I don't understand," confessed Nattie. "How will that keep my presence a secret from her?"

"You're going to be her new publicist."

Before Nattie could respond, Kevin said, "That's perfect. Her publicist would have full access to her."

Smiling, Roberta tipped her head toward Kevin. "I'm glad you approve."

"I'm glad you approve too, Kevin," added Nattie. Then to the Farmers she said, "We accept. One of our staff will pose as Knox's new publicist. When is her next engagement?"

"There's a place in Sylva called O'Malley's. She's playing there on Saturday."

"Sylva?"

"It's in North Carolina, about twenty minutes from Cherokee," said Mel.

"We had already scheduled to go to Cherokee for the weekend," Roberta said as she opened her purse again. Taking out a folded sheet of paper, Roberta continued, "This is our itinerary, but I think it would be better if we could introduce Knox to her new publicist before we go over to Cherokee."

"If she's going to meet her new publicist before you leave for Cherokee, that means this afternoon or tomorrow morning," observed Nattie. "How about we make it a breakfast meeting tomorrow?"

"That's great," Mel said as he stood. "Now that that's settled, can I get back to work?"

Roberta stood up also. "Yes, Mel, go back to work. I have an appointment, too." She turned to Nattie: "Can we meet at Perkins in the morning?"

Nodding yes, Nattie answered, "Someone from our staff will be there at nine o'clock."

Mel took a folded check from his pocket and handed it to Kevin. "This will more than cover the retainer."

"Listen, folks," said Kevin in a serious voice that Nattie had never heard. "We don't want you to worry anymore. Natasha is the best there is."

Nattie frowned at him. "We already have the job, Kevin."

"Come on, Natasha," said Kevin, sounding like Rex Harrison from *My Fair Lady*, "this is no time for false humidity."

CHAPTER 4

Kevin

Rolling his chair back to his desk, Kevin watched the Farmers through the office window. After a peck on the lips, Mel Farmer stepped into his silver Cadillac while Roberta walked across the parking lot toward Machiavelli's. Turning back to Nattie, Kevin stated, "I thought that went well. They seem like good people, don't you think?"

"I'm not sure, *Agent* Johnson," answered Nattie from the doorway to her office. "When did you become an agent?" Without waiting for him to answer she asked, "What is an agent, anyway? Do they think you're some kind of a spy?"

"They think I work here. They think they can talk to me about agency stuff. That makes me an agent, doesn't it?"

Nattie stepped closer to the window and watched Roberta enter Machiavelli's.

"You didn't answer my question. Don't you think they are good people?"

Squinting, Nattie said, "I don't know, Kevin. Maybe they are. Don't you think it's a little weird to refer to your daughter by her stage name rather than the name you gave her?"

"I didn't think about it. I guess she's just proud of her daughter's success."

"That's another thing. She said her daughter was in show business."

"Well, what's wrong with that? She is in show business. Sometimes, Nattie, I think you are too suspicious."

"She's a lounge singer, and of course that is show business, but referring to her that way is misleading."

"She's proud of her daughter," Kevin shrugged. "She's putting her in the best light."

"Maybe," said Nattie. "But I wonder if Candy feels her life is acceptable as it is when her mother feels the need to exaggerate it."

"So, you don't really think she is good people," Kevin tried again.

Nattie stared silently at nothing out the window.

"Why'd you take the job, Sis?"

Sighing, "I needed something to do. And I think Candy Farmer may need my help in more ways than one."

"Yes, that's right. You're going to be her publicist, too."

"Speaking of that, you've heard her sing right, Kevin?"

"Yeah, a couple of times. Why?"

"I was just curious. What's she like?"

Kevin thought a moment, then scratched his head. "I don't know how old she is, but she looks like a thirteen-year-old Sarah Jessica Parker and dresses like Annie Hall."

"And you said she sounds like Alison Krause."

"I did. She sounds *almost* like Alison Krause. Almost."

"What does 'almost' mean, Kevin?"

"Well, she sounds exactly like Alison . . . when she hits the notes."

"Oh my."

"Yeah, it's pretty bad. I wish someone would tell her to avoid songs that are just too high for her. Hey," Kevin exclaimed, pointing, "maybe her new publicist could do that."

Nattie smiled at him. "You'll have to let me know how that works out."

After a minute Kevin hocked his thumbs around imaginary suspenders. "I'm the publicist?" he bragged.

"Why not? You're an agent of the agency, aren't you?"

A serious look crossed Kevin's face as he looked down at the top of his desk. "You know, being her publicist might be kind of fun. What exactly does a publicist do? Is it like being her agent?"

"No, I'm pretty sure Roberta is her agent, and I'm pretty sure she's not gonna give that position up."

"So what does an agent do? Make the deals?"

"I think that's exactly what an agent does. The publicist does the advertising."

"I could do that," Kevin boasted. "I could start by asking what her last publicist did and didn't do. That way she can tell me what she wants me to do. What do you think?"

"I'd say your first task is to convince Knox that you are in fact a publicist."

Kevin's eyes lit up, which usually meant that the wheels of his imagination were in gear. "I could tell her about all the products I've handled. There's the *First Timer's Guide to Italy,* Ain't Miss Bee Haven Honey, and," pointing at Nattie, "there's that cookbook I'm developing with Ollie Ruggiliano."

Great, Kevin, she thought as she watched him rev up. *Go ahead and tell her about every harebrained idea you've ever had.*

"There's Coffee Jelly and the Beginner's Coin Collecting Kit," he continued.

Having unleashed Kevin's creative mind, Nattie could do nothing more but get out of the way. She headed for the door. Her mother was waiting across the way at Machiavelli's.

As the door closed behind Nattie, Kevin continued the list of products he could claim to have handled. "And of course," he said, "there's Dirty Diaper in a Bowl."

CHAPTER 5

Lunch with Ingrid

NATTIE FOUND HER MOTHER RIGHT AWAY as she entered Machiavelli's. Ingrid was sitting in one of the booths along the left wall. After a quick glance into the larger dining room she took the seat across from her mother. She could see Roberta Farmer' s back from where she sat. With the contrast of her mother nearby and Roberta at a distance, it became clearer to Natalie why she was so put off by the latter. Roberta was as authoritative in her daughter's life as Ingrid was permissive in Natalie's. *Am I jealous?* Natalie wondered, then shuddered at the notion of being under that much control.

"What's good here?" asked Ingrid, closing the book she was reading.

"Do you want what Kevin orders here or what I order here?"

"I'll bet I could guess what Kevin orders here. It's the Italian nachos. Am I right?"

"Yes. What was the tip-off?"

"That's easy. I just looked for the most unusual combination of the things he likes: nachos, sausage, and Alfredo sauce."

"And me?" Nattie asked and immediately regretted it. She doubted Ingrid would have the same insight about her daughter as she did about her son. *Roberta would know what Candy would want because Roberta would order it for her.*

"You are much harder to predict, Nattie."

And I know why.

"Because," continued Ingrid, "for you quality is important. So I'd say that the brick-oven pizza is one of your favorites, but only if it's good."

Not bad, thought Nattie.

"But, for lunch, my guess is one of the salads."

"You're right," conceded Nattie. "I am harder to please than Kevin. Quantity is more important to him than it is to me, but my favorite thing on the menu is the glazed pears with blue cheese and caramelized onions. My next favorite thing is the same as Kevin's, the Italian nachos. Actually, Mother, my tastes and Kevin's are pretty close. The only difference between us is that he always eats what he wants and I don't, but generally speaking I want what he wants."

The waitress came to the table. "Do you know what you want, or do you need another minute?"

Ingrid looked across the table. "When you don't order what you want here, what do you order?"

"The Greek salad."

Ingrid held up two fingers to the waitress. "And two waters with lime."

"Have you read this?" asked Ingrid, tapping the book in front of her.

"I don't know. What is it?"

"*A Rising Son* by Craig McDonald. Isn't he the King College professor you went with to England?"

"He is. That must be his latest book. Is it set in Scotland, too?"

Looking at the cover . . . "No, this one is set in biblical times."

"Are you enjoying it?" asked Nattie.

"I am. I think it would be a good book for you, too."

"Why? What's it about?"

"It's about a lot of things, but one is that it's about dying well."

Nattie's whole body stiffened. The realization of where her mother was directing the conversation hit her like a bolt.

Reaching across the table Ingrid placed her hand on top of Nattie's. "I didn't mean to startle you, sweetheart. I just know you're having a hard time."

"I'm fine," reacted Nattie quickly.

"You aren't fine, Nattie. I mention death, and you freeze. You're still holding your breath."

"I'm handling it."

"You may not want to hear this, but, darling daughter, you and I are cut from the same cloth."

Nattie returned her mother's attention with a sideways look of her own. "What does that mean?"

"It means you're as tough as nails."

Nattie tipped her head even more to the side.

"I'm talking about how we handle pain, dear. I know you think I am a weakling when it comes to men."

"I never said that."

"You've never needed to say that," Ingrid laughed. "I know you don't approve of my relationship with Lionel."

"That's not true, Mother."

"It may not be true now, but it sure was in the beginning. Come on, Nattie, admit it."

"Okay. I didn't approve then. You completely changed who you were in order to catch and keep him."

"Honey, don't confuse behavior with reality. I used the assets available to me to accomplish what I needed to accomplish to take care of myself and my two kids."

"You completely abandoned your affection for St. Francis to please him."

30

"Did I?" Ingrid asked. "Are you sure?"

Nattie hesitated. "I retrieved all your St. Francis stuff from the trash just before we moved in with him."

Ingrid reached inside her blouse and lifted the slender gold chain until it revealed the St. Francis cross at the end. "You didn't get all of it."

For the second time that day Nattie saw something unexpected from the mother she thought she had figured out long ago. "I'm not sure I know who you are."

"That's not your job, Nattie. You're not my mother. I'm your mother. And right now your mother wants to know how you are. I mean I want to know how you really are."

Nattie stalled by glancing at Roberta in the other room again. Without looking she said, "Why would God do that to her?"

"God didn't kill Marissa."

"But he let it happen. She was the most religious person I've ever known. She might have been the most moral, most ethical person I've ever known. Why should she have to die?"

"I don't know how to answer a question like that. Would you like to talk to Lionel?"

"Not really," responded Nattie quickly.

"Why not, Nattie?"

The strained relationship between Nattie and her stepfather started badly when Ingrid married him six months after they met. The strain grew progressively worse until the end of Nattie's sophomore year of college, when her choice to major in psychology resulted in Ingrid and Lionel withholding financial support. Their relationship had improved tremendously a few years afterward when a lawyer who worked at Lionel's law firm roadblocked Nattie's investigation of a murder. Lionel had started out supporting his lawyer, but he came through for Nattie in the end. In spite of having a much-improved understanding in most ways, Nattie still considered Lionel to be a fundamentalist right-wing religious zealot, an opinion she was not about to share with Ingrid.

"She was my friend, Mother. I was holding her when she died. I'm just not in the mood to listen to Lionel give me some pat answer from his Sunday school class."

"Oh, Nattie, I can't believe you said that. He's much more complicated than that."

Nattie looked toward Roberta in the other room again. There seemed to be no end to the gaiety at that table.

"You were away at school when my parents died in that car crash," began Ingrid.

The statement brought Nattie's full attention back to the table.

"It was a million times harder on me than when your father left us. It was so unexpected. I was so unprepared." It was Ingrid's turn to look away. "I was just like you. At first I was strong, you know, but then I started to get irritable, sleeping all the time." Facing Nattie again, "Lionel was great. He just let me wallow for a while, and when he thought I was ready he talked to me."

"Did he tell you that you were showing a lack of faith?"

Ingrid ignored Nattie's sarcasm. "No, what he told me was how he felt when his first wife died."

Nattie did not notice her own shoulders dropping lower or her fist unclenching. She was aware of leaning forward against the table and holding her hand out alongside her mother's.

Stroking the back of Nattie's hand, Ingrid continued. "He told me that he'd go to work all day and act strong, and then he'd come home in the evening and be strong for Samantha, who was just a kid then. And then, late at night, when he was alone, he let himself fall apart."

They looked at each other silently for a moment before Ingrid said, "He gave me permission to cry."

Nattie could feel the temperature rise behind her eyes. "I'm glad he was there for you, Mom," she said tenderly—then, with a deep slow breath, "I'm sorry I talked so harshly about him before. He's your husband. It wasn't right for me to say those things to you."

"Oh, Nattie, you don't have to apologize for thinking he's a blowhard. He is a blowhard. But I wish you could see that that's not all he is."

Snickering, "So, Mom, did he eventually give you advice?"

"Three things," answered Ingrid with three fingers in the air. "One: When it's time to work, cowboy up and work. Two: When it's not time to work, let yourself fall apart. Three—well, three isn't advice so much as it's wisdom."

"What did he say?" Nattie's question had a sincerity to it that would have surprised her had she not been so focused.

"He said I'd never be able to answer the why questions I was asking, and that the only way to get past those questions was to begin asking, 'What now?'"

While holding on to her mother's hand, Nattie said, "Thanks, Mom. I guess I needed a kick in the butt."

"Aw, we all need an occasional kick in the butt," Ingrid smiled. "What you needed was a little girl to protect."

Their Greek salads came and went as they discussed various points of interest about Cherokee, North Carolina. After clearing their dishes the waitress came back with what Nattie assumed would be the check.

"What's this?" asked Nattie as the waitress placed a plate with two glazed pears on the table between them.

As the waitress gave each of them clean forks Ingrid said, "I told her to bring this as a dessert when I first saw it on the menu."

"Not before she made sure the pears were fresh," added the waitress.

CHAPTER 6

Nathan

"I THOUGHT YOU ASKED ME OVER," stated Nathan defiantly.

"I did."

Lifting his left arm he made sure she could see that it was eleven thirty on his watch. "I thought this would be a sleepover."

"I'm not ready for that kind of sleepover. I thought we made that clear," said Nattie firmly. She had divorced him because he was an out-of-control alcoholic who refused to take responsibility for his life. She didn't know that he was an alcoholic when she married him, but it made sense that she would marry one. She, being the caretaker from her own alcoholic family of origin, gravitated toward men who needed care. But Nathan's irresponsibility taxed even her capacity for overre-sponsibility. She still loved him, so when she agreed to begin dating him again she made him agree to a set of rules that were designed to keep her desires in check as much as his.

"I know," he said looking down. "I just thought you were ready to break the rule." Grinning he added, "You know I'm ready."

Nattie stared at him without smiling. When his grin disappeared she said, "I'm sorry if you were led on, and I wouldn't blame you if you decided to go home. But I need you."

"What?" he asked with a softer tone. Taking hold of each of her upper arms he hunched down to be more at eye level with her. "Just tell me, Nat. I'll do anything for you."

Laying her head against his chest Nattie stepped into his embrace and circled her arms around his middle. They stood holding each other for several minutes before Nattie broke the silence. "Thank you, Nathan."

"You're welcome, Nattie. I want to be the guy you call for this."

I want that too, she thought.

"Do you want to talk?"

"That would be nice, but not tonight. What I was hoping you'd be willing to do is watch a movie with me."

Pulling his head back for a better look at her face, he knit his eyebrows together.

"I'm going to start getting busy again. In fact, I'll be leaving for Cherokee tomorrow. So tonight what I need is to have a good cry."

Nathan's confused look remained. "And you want to watch a movie?"

"I know, it sounds silly, but the last time I had a good cry was when we watched *The Pursuit of Happiness.* I was hoping that would do it again."

"Okay, Nat. If you think that will help you, then I'm in. Do you want me to make another fire?"

She shook her head no. "I think just watching the movie is enough."

But it was not enough. They settled onto Nattie's couch in the same positions they were in the first time they watched the movie. That was the day after Marissa had died. Nathan sat to Nattie's right with his arm around her while Nattie rested her head on his chest with her left arm around his waist. Her feelings were raw and close to the surface that night. The movie had been mostly background as her focus was hypnotically drawn to the fire, while her attention shifted rapidly from one intruding memory to another. The scene in the movie that triggered her tears was the scene in which the father, homeless and broke, locked himself and his son in a bathroom and cried as his son slept on his lap. Although she had seen the movie before, the scene was as unexpected as was its effect.

Nathan had taken his place at the left end of the couch while Nattie was starting the movie and turning out most of the lights. Instead of snuggling up under his arm, she simply lay on the couch, resting her head on his left thigh. Their interest in the movie, having just watched it six weeks earlier, was not enough to curtail the restlessness in Nathan's leg or Nattie's irritation at him for moving. Putting a small pillow between her head and his leg helped, but not enough to settle her own restlessness, which took the form of distraction.

This isn't working, she ruminated. *What was I thinking? What is he thinking?*

Taking a deep breath she focused her attention on the movie by sheer assertion of will. In anticipation of the bathroom scene she began to create her own images. She determined it would be Marissa she would picture being held in the father's lap. As the scene approached, her efforts to force her version of the scene into her imagination increased. When the moment finally came and the scene she had waited for appeared on the screen she held her breath, steeling her body the way one would do as a roller-coaster car approached the crest of the first incline.

The scene came and went with virtually no effect other than her awareness that she had been holding her breath again. She stared blankly at the television for a few more minutes before sitting up.

"What's the matter?" asked Nathan.

She patted his hand. "It's not you. You were great. Thanks for being here. I guess I'm just not ready."

He kept his eyes on her but didn't speak.

It's good that he's not trying to fix me, Nattie thought appreciatively. "I think we need to call it a night."

He nodded and stood up. "I'm glad you called me, Nat. I'm sorry it didn't work the way you wanted, but I love that I'm the one you called."

That was a homerun, she noted to herself. Standing up next to him she put her arm around his waist. "Come on, I'll walk you to the door."

On her front step he turned into her embrace and held her against himself, resting the side of his head on top of hers. "Are you going to be okay?"

Squeezing his middle, "I am."

"And you leave for Cherokee tomorrow, right?"

"Yeah, why?"

"I was just thinking that if you were going to go through Weaverville, I could follow you and we could eat at the Stoney Knob again."

She leaned back to look up at his face. "If you want to do that, we could drive over together and Kevin could drive your car there, then you could drive it back to Bristol."

"Kevin's going with you?"

"He's posing as a publicist for a singer," Nattie grinned.

"I'll bet he's getting into that."

"You know him. When he's in, he's all in."

"Tomorrow then," he said before kissing her on the forehead and ambling to his car at the street.

Nattie stood, arms wrapped around her middle, watching him drive off until his car was out of sight. Then she went inside, locked the front door, turned off everything downstairs, and headed up to her bedroom.

Normally she was an excellent sleeper. The only time she was restless as she slept was when it was hot and humid. Going to sleep was rarely a problem either, but occasionally she would have a hard time, almost always associated with caffeine. Although she did not have any caffeine that evening, too much caffeine was what she felt as she closed her eyes.

She was too exhausted to get up, and she knew that if she opened her eyes, even for a moment, she would be wide awake. So she kept her eyes closed and turned to her yoga breathing skills. Mindful breathing usually helped calm her. After a few minutes of deep rhythmic breathing she still could not sleep, but she was relaxing more and more. Letting her mind drift where it would, she began thinking about Nathan and how sweet he had been. She missed him, but she was still afraid to let herself want him too much.

This time when the fantasy of being held by him drifted into her awareness, she did not fight it off. Pictures of standing with him on her front steps morphed into pictures of snuggling up against him on the couch. As the pictures wafted through her mind she unconsciously embraced her pillow.

Something changed as she relaxed. She began to picture the bathroom scene from the movie again. Her breathing grew heavy as the bathroom came into focus. The picture in her mind was moving as if it were a camera focusing first on the background and then on the father's feet. As the camera angle moved across the father's prone body, the warmth behind her eyes increased. The lump growing in her throat went unnoticed as the camera moved to the father's head. It was her own face Nattie saw, and she was holding Marissa. They were no longer in the bathroom but in that parking lot across from Manna Bagel. But it was not Marissa the camera framed. It was Nattie. And then it happened. She could not have stopped it if she tried. All she could do was turn her head into the pillow to muffle the sounds she had never heard.

Part 2

CHEROKEE

CHAPTER 7

Benjamin Walls

"Is this what Kevin calls 'Tomato Soup Row'?" asked Ingrid as they hiked from Nattie's office to the Benjamin Walls Gallery. They were on the Virginia side of State Street.

Nattie had to think a moment before it dawned on her what Ingrid was referring to. She guessed that it must be some goofy thing Kevin had said. Sure enough it was. "Yes, Mom, Kevin calls this 'Tomato Soup Row' because of all the varieties of tomato soup you can get along here."

Nattie stopped across from KP Duty. "On Tuesdays that place specializes in tomato bisque." Then turning to face Ingrid she asked, "Do you remember the place directly across from my office?"

"You mean where we just had lunch?" said Ingrid sarcastically.

An embarrassed grin flashed across Nattie's face. "Yes, where we just had lunch. That's Machiavelli's, and their tomato soup special is tomato Florentine."

As Nattie began walking again she cupped her mother's elbow with her right hand and pointed down the street with her left hand. "And down there at Manna Bagel they serve a tomato basil soup."

"That is a lot of variety," agreed Ingrid.

"Well, that's not all. The Bistro, which is a couple of blocks beyond where we're going, has a tomato soup with thyme."

Leaning toward her daughter as they kept walking Ingrid asked, "You might not remember this, but when you and Kevin were little I used to make you tomato soup."

"We remember."

"It was just Campbell's out of a can, but I used to make these open-faced grilled cheese sandwiches, too."

"I remember, Momma," said Nattie as she squeezed her mother's arm against her side. "With tomato and onion."

Ingrid's eyes lit up with the mention of her special sandwich.

"Kevin even got the Manna Bagel people to make a bagel sandwich like that. And guess what he named it?"

"Momma's Special?" Ingrid guessed.

"Exactly," said Nattie, in spite of the fact that it was really called "the Natasha" after her.

They continued weaving their way down the street.

"Thanks for tagging along, Momma."

"Thanks for asking me," said Ingrid. "Was there a particular reason you wanted me to come with you?"

"Nope. I just enjoyed lunch so much that I wanted to take advantage of this kind of activity to hang out more. It's not very often a PI can invite her mother to tag along."

Ingrid squeezed Nattie's arm as they walked. "I really enjoyed lunch, too," she said with a smile.

Without really knowing why, Nattie asked, "Mother, did you want me to have another reason?"

Ingrid's head pivoted back and forth, and she squinted as she shook her head no.

"Mother," said Nattie, motherly.

A deep inhale. Eyes focused down the street. "I don't know," Ingrid said. "I just thought it might be fun to be your decorator or purchasing agent."

A few minutes later they walked into Benjamin Walls Fine Art Gallery.

"Wow," said Ingrid as she looked at the huge photo of the snow-covered trees facing the door. "I think I'll just browse around while you do your thing."

As Nattie turned to go toward the back of the shop, Ben strolled by, opening a pair of aviator sunglasses.

"You're Benjamin Walls, aren't you?" asked Nattie.

He removed the sunglasses he had just put on. "I am. Can I help you?"

"I hope so," she said. "I need to pick your brain, if that's okay."

His eyebrows scrunched together as he studied her.

"I'm Nattie Moreland," she introduced herself. "I'm a detective. My office is about four blocks down State Street from yours."

He shook hands with her. "That's interesting. There's another detective down there." Scratching his head, "She got a real unusual name."

"Natasha McMorales," offered Ingrid, joining them.

"That sounds right," he said.

"That's me," Nattie said. "I mean, I'm her. I mean . . . I'm Nattie Moreland. Natasha McMorales is the name of my agency."

"Are you Natasha?" Ben asked Ingrid.

"No, I'm not, but I am her mother."

Ignoring Ingrid as she stepped too close to him he turned to Nattie. "I have to hit the road in about an hour, so right now I'm going to get something to eat. If you want to pick my brain you are welcome to come with me. Would that work?"

"If it is okay with you, it's okay with us," answered Ingrid as she took hold of his arm and led him toward the door.

Nattie followed two steps behind Ben and Ingrid as they crossed the street and entered CityMug.

"So, Ben," Nattie could hear her mother say, "you have heard of my daughter."

"I have."

"Did you read about one of her cases in the paper?"

"Not exactly."

"Well, how exactly have you heard of her?"

By the time she asked her last question, Ingrid and Ben were standing at the order counter.

"I know her because of this," he said, pointing at the sandwiches.

Ingrid scanned the counter but saw nothing that explained his statement.

"I'll have a Natasha Panini," he said to Jana, one of the baristas behind the counter, as he watched for Ingrid's reaction.

"There's a sandwich here named after my daughter?" marveled Ingrid.

He nodded yes.

"Why didn't you say anything to me, Nattie?"

"Because I didn't know," answered Nattie. "I'm sure Kevin set it up."

"Oh yeah," interjected Jana. "It was Kevin's idea. He invented the sandwich."

"Is it a grilled cheese sandwich?" asked Ingrid.

"It is," explained Rebekah, who was standing behind Jana. "It's a panini with mozzarella cheese, tomato, and pesto. It's Ben's favorite sandwich."

"I'll bring it out to you when it's ready," said Jana as she began working on his lunch.

Ben led them to the front and sat in the upholstered chair facing the window. "So, Nattie, how can I help you?"

After Nattie and her mother settled in on the adjacent couch, Nattie scooted forward and explained, "I've been hired to protect someone from a stalker and I have to follow her without her knowing what I'm doing. I thought I could pretend to be a photographer. I was hoping you could give me a couple of tips so I could pass myself off as a professional photographer."

43

After gazing out of the window for a moment he said, "Make sure you use film cameras. If you use digital cameras people are going to want to see what you are doing right away. That way you can stall and say it has to be developed first."

"I hadn't thought of that," admitted Nattie.

"And," he continued, "it will look more authentic if you carry a lot of equipment, too. I can lend you some old stuff of mine if you need it."

"You'd do that for me?"

"Sure. When do you need it?"

"I leave for Cherokee tomorrow," answered Nattie.

"No problem. Drop by the gallery sometime tomorrow, and I'll have a bag set up and ready to go for you."

Jana brought his sandwich to him and sat it on the coffee table.

"Thank you very much, Ben," said Nattie as she stood and extended her hand. "I appreciate your help. We'll let you have your lunch in peace."

"No problem," he said with a grin. "Just don't get too good at taking pictures."

CHAPTER 8

Thursday: Weaverville

"I'M CURIOUS, NATTIE," NATHAN SAID as soon as the Stoney Knob Café hostess left their table.

"What's on your mind, Nathan?" Nattie asked over the top of her menu while removing her sunglasses and setting them on the table.

"Don't get me wrong," he began. "I loved that you told me all about the case you are working on while we were driving."

She waited for him to continue, but it appeared he believed it was her turn to speak.

"But . . . ," she finally said after waiting longer than she thought reasonable to hear about his curiosity.

"But you've never done that before."

We used to do it all the time before your second DUI lost you your PI license, she thought but did not say.

"It felt good to be included," he continued, "but I don't understand what has changed."

"Are you suggesting that I'm violating the PI code of ethics?" She realized immediately that her attempt to kid him was off target because his eyes blinked several times and his lips moved slightly without making any sound. "Relax, Nathan, I know you weren't accusing me."

He sighed, exhaling loudly.

"Boy, I guess I've really done a number on you, haven't I?"

"What do you mean?" he asked.

"I mean, I've been so hot and cold with you that you nearly have a heart attack when I give you a little zing."

His looking back at her with a blank stare and a slightly raised eyebrow told her that he agreed with her assessment.

"I'm sorry," she said. Placing her hand atop his, she continued, "I don't think I've thanked you enough for the past few weeks. You've been real sweet to me, and I really appreciate it."

"Hi, I'm Janine, and I'll be your server." The voice came from a thirty-something waitress who wore her dark hair pulled back in a tight ponytail. "I can come back in a minute if you'd like," she said as she noticed that Nathan had not taken his eyes off Nattie's hand when Janine had announced her presence at the table. The line was delivered with a straight face, as if it were a straightforward statement, yet she made not the slightest move to leave. Janine's neck was unusually long—at least it seemed long with her hair gathered behind her head—and she had the ability to pull her head back without moving her shoulders. The effect gave the waitress the appearance of detached amusement regarding whatever caught her attention. This was the look Nathan saw when he finally looked up from his stupor.

Nattie placed her order. "I'll have the crab cakes and the gorgonzola slaw. And water with lime."

Janine nodded, tucked Nattie's menu under her arm, and turned toward Nathan without writing anything down. "And you, sir?"

Opening his menu for the first time, Nathan ran his finger down the sandwich menu and began to talk out loud. "I've had that burger at lunch, and I don't think it's worth that much." Realizing what he had just said he looked sheepishly at Janine.

"You didn't have that burger at lunch. That's the Big Ass Kobe Burger," Janine responded. "It's just a dinner item."

"When I told Kevin we were coming here for dinner, he recommended the burger," added Nattie.

"How many stars?" asked Nathan.

Nattie held up five fingers.

"Really, Kevin said five stars," said Nathan out loud and to himself.

Kevin was a burger connoisseur. He had a business card that said so. On Kevin's scale, five stars meant excellence in meat quality, meat size, bun quality, extras, and presentation. Extras were the combinations of garnishes, condiments, and whatever else was added beyond the meat and the bun. Presentation for Kevin included what the plate looked like, what the place looked like, and how engaging the service was.

When Nathan finally looked up and told Janine he wanted the burger, she nodded like she had just been patiently waiting for him to realize what both women already knew.

"And that Kalamazoo Stout with licorice, is it a strong licorice taste?"

"I have no idea," answered Janine.

He shrugged. "I'll try it."

Janine came back with their drinks, a basket of Italian bread, and a dish of olive oil and herbs. Nattie's water was in an insulated metal glass, which she loved because it kept her water cold. While she squeezed her lime into her water Nathan swabbed a piece of bread in the olive oil. After licking the oil from his lips he took a long draw from his beer. "Not bad," he declared. "Just a hint of licorice."

Nattie cleared her throat in an attempt to draw his attention. When he looked up she asked, "Have you ever heard Knox DeVilla sing?"

"Knox! Is that who you were talking about on the way over here?"

"I take it that you know her."

"I don't really know her, but she's been to Our House a few times."

Shaking his head he added, "So, little Knox has a stalker. I can't say I'm surprised."

Nathan's statement perked Nattie up. "Tell me more."

"Have you seen her?" he asked.

"No, why?"

"I'd guess she's in her twenties, but she looks like she's in her teens. When she's on she comes across as a shy surfer girl with a sweet voice, dreadlocks, and a nice figure." He stopped, looking across the table waiting for Nattie to respond.

"Are you telling me that her looks might be inviting a stalker?"

He shrugged. "When she sings at Our House there's always a lot more middle-aged men that come in. And I don't think it's because she such a good musician."

"So she's selling sex," snarled Nattie.

"No, Nattie," he said with a wave of his hands. "I didn't mean to make it sound like that. I don't think she's aware of her effect on those men. In fact I'm sure she doesn't know. When she performs she's oblivious to the audience. It doesn't seem like she's comfortable acknowledging that there's anyone else in the room."

Janine appeared with their meals. As she sat Nathan's Big Ass Kobe Burger down, she waited for his response. The burger was huge, dwarfing the little metal cup that held the fries in a bouquet instead of a pile. Looking up he found both women watching him. "Is that all there is?"

Janine pulled her head back. A trace of a smile appeared as she turned to go. That was all the answer he was going to get to his question.

"Did you notice that thing she does with her head?"

"What thing?"

He tried to extend his neck and pull his head back.

"Okay," she said with a chuckle. "I've seen her do that."

"Well, I don't notice her doing that to you."

Nattie smiled. "And why would she do that to me?"

"Why is she doing it to me?" he countered.

"Maybe she has you pegged as a little boy trying to get a reaction."

It took a moment for him to decide that being called a little boy was not an insult. With a grin he drained the last of the stout from his glass.

As he put his empty glass down, Janine stopped at the edge of the table. In her hands she held two plates of food for another table. "Do you want another one?"

His eyes moved from Janine to his empty glass and finally across the table to Nattie. "No thanks."

Why the look, Nathan? wondered Nattie. *Were you looking for permission to have another or credit for not?*

He carefully cut his burger in half and then, after taking a healthy bite, he nodded his agreement to Kevin's assessment.

Nattie gave him time to enjoy his first bite and then asked, "Can you think of any particular middle-aged man who might be her stalker?"

"No, but I can check with Al and Britt if you want. They were tending bar the last time she was there."

"Thanks. Any other thoughts?"

He put his burger down and wiped his mouth—a cue that he was going to be serious. "Didn't you tell me that the note from the stalker connected her to those two WXBQ disc jockeys?"

"Yes."

"Well, doesn't that mean that whoever killed them is the one threatening her?"

"It could mean that, but it could be that the stalker was just using those murders to scare her."

"Of course," he agreed, as he reassembled his burger.

49

"Have you had any dealings with her folks?"

"Not her dad, but her mother is her business manager. I've dealt with her."

"Do you have any red flags about her?"

"Not really," he shrugged. "She does most of the talking. It always seemed a little off when she would answer questions I asked Knox, but that's about it. You don't suspect she's got something to do with it, do you?"

"Anything's possible. It could be a play for publicity. Or she could be a drama junkie." Nattie cut an edge off one of her crab cakes and held it up before admitting, "I don't know what it is, but something about her really rubs me the wrong way."

Nathan looked at Nattie like he had never heard her speak this way about anyone.

Their concentration on their respective meals was then only occasionally interrupted by references to the quality, the quantity, and several attempts by each of them to get the other to sample what they were eating.

Kevin, who had followed them in Nathan's Mustang and eaten at the Well Bred Bakery, pulled into the parking place on the other side of the window from where they sat. Nattie watched him step out of the car and stretch.

"There's just one more thing I want to tell you before Kevin gets in here."

Having just put the last big bite of his Big Ass Burger into his mouth, Nathan acknowledged her statement by nodding his head.

"I have no idea if this case is legit or not, but if it is I'm going to need more help."

Nathan stopped chewing. She had his undivided attention.

"So," she continued, "can I call on you if I need you?"

In his excitement he had difficulty deciding how to respond. He wanted to say, "Of course," but the bite in his mouth was too big. He tentatively tried to swallow, but the bite in his mouth was too big for that as well. Spitting was the most efficient solution he could think of, so, without noticing that Janine had returned, he tipped his head over his plate and out dropped the last remnant of his dinner.

Janine, who was in the process of lifting his empty plate, stared at it with no change of expression. She managed to pull her head back on her neck a bit more. Turning slowly to Nathan, she said, "Are you finished with that, sir?"

CHAPTER 9

The Drive to Cherokee

"Wow," said Kevin as Nattie settled in behind the wheel of her Subaru Forester. It was parked close to the street in the Stoney Knob parking lot. She had just said good-bye to Nathan, whose car was next to the front door.

" 'Wow,' what?" she asked.

"Not a bad 'wow,' " he explained. "A good 'wow.' " Then he smiled one of those I-know-a-secret smiles, which made Nattie roll her eyes and turn her attention to starting her car.

"I think it's nice," he said.

She inched her car forward and looked to the left for oncoming traffic. Seeing none, she pulled out onto Weaverville Highway headed toward Asheville.

"Don't you want to know what I think is nice?" he asked.

Does it matter? she asked herself.

"I'm glad you and Nathan are getting along now."

"Look, Kevin," she began, "I don't want you to make a big deal out of this, but Nathan and I have been spending a lot of time together." Then, glaring at him, she added, "But I don't want Mom to know until I want her to know. Do you understand?"

He laughed.

"Are you forgetting I have a gun?"

"Easy, sheriff," he said, holding his hands up in surrender. "I was just laughing at the idea that you don't want Mom to know."

"Why is that funny?"

He looked at her with scrunched eyebrows as if trying to determine if she was serious. "Are you thinking that Mom doesn't already know Nathan has been taking care of you since . . . ?" He did not finish his thought on the death of Marissa.

"Nathan hasn't been taking care of me," she said too quickly to be believable.

Keeping his eyes on the road ahead he said, "Well, Mom knows that Nathan has been spending significant time with you lately."

"Aw, Kevin," she whined.

"Hey, Sis, don't blame me. She went over to your house last week with all the fixings to make you tomato soup and her onion and tomato grilled-cheese sandwiches."

"I didn't know that."

"Of course not. She saw Nathan's 'stang and decided to leave you alone."

"How did she know it was Nathan's Mustang?"

The right side of Kevin's mouth flinched. "She called me," he said slowly as he tightened up in anticipation of a punch.

"So, you did tell her."

"All I did was answer her question. If she had gone in she'd have found out herself." He wagged a finger at her. "You can't blame me for that."

"I suppose you're right."

With that he grinned and relaxed his shoulders, and then she hit him in the chest.

Normally Nattie had a hard time doing anything slowly. Once she had a goal in mind she gave very little time or attention to anything other than the goal. The effect of this approach to life was that she generally accomplished whatever she put her mind to, but another effect was that she often missed out on enjoying the journey. To compensate for her hurry-up tendency she sometimes played mind games with herself. She knew that, left to her own devices, the trip to Cherokee would be a blur followed by several hours of boredom in a motel room. Instead she set an explicit goal of a leisurely trip through Western North Carolina.

They shared stories about Asheville as they took the I-240 bypass around the northern edge of the city. They agreed on their favorite restaurant, Salsa's, but for Kevin his favorite item was the enchiladas, while Nattie loved the Ginger-Hibiscus iced tea.

"All that talk about food makes me hungry," announced Kevin.

"Didn't you just eat?"

"Yes, but I didn't have dessert." Twisting he reached between their seats to the floorboard behind Nattie. "Do you want a cookie?" he asked as he retrieved a white paper bag from the Well Bred Bakery.

"What do you have?"

"Orange chocolate chip," he said with a crooked grin. "And I got one for you. Are you ready?"

"Not now, but since you got one for me I'll save it for later, thanks. Tell me about your meeting this morning."

"It went well. I'm pretty sure she bought that I'm a publicist."

"Pretty sure?" Nattie asked.

"Well, as sure as anyone could be. Knox is hard to read."

"You call her 'Knox'?"

"Sure. Why not?"

"Her real name is Candy. Knox is her stage name."

"They all called her 'Knox.' Even Phyllis, her grandmother, calls her 'Knox.' She's got a Facebook page with the name 'Knox.'"

"That's for publicity, right?"

"No. It's her personal page. She doesn't use Facebook for promotion." He took a big bite of cookie, then mumbled, "In fact, that was my angle as a publicist. I'm going to help her set up a musician page and events."

"That's good, Kevin."

Smiling broadly revealed the remnants of orange-chocolate cookie across his front teeth. "It gives me a justification to know about her whole schedule, not just her performances."

"Great. Is there anything I need to know about her schedule?"

"They've got the grandmother with them, so the plan was to take her to the casino tonight. Friday morning they're going to a museum, and then of course she's on at O'Malley's in Sylva on Friday night. Then Saturday night they have tickets to a play. That's it as far as I know."

"You've got the names of the museum and the play, right? I don't want to be in the wrong place."

"The Museum of the Cherokee Indian, and the play is *Unto These Hills.* She posted both of those on her Facebook page."

Nattie scowled. "Do you mean she announced to the world where she was going to be?"

"She did."

"Oh, great," Nattie fumed. "This is why I don't like the idea of her not being in the know about all of this. How am I supposed to protect her if she does stuff like that?"

"I didn't think you agreed to protect her anyway. You told her parents you weren't set up for that. They don't expect you to protect her. As a matter of fact I don't think they believe she needs protection."

"Really?"

"Yeah. Mr. Farmer is convinced Knox sent that note herself."

"And Mrs. Farmer?"

"I don't get the idea that she's worried about it, but she won't hear of backing off either."

"How about you, Kevin? Do you think Knox could have sent the note herself?"

"No," answered Kevin without hesitation. "I don't think she's that kind of person." After a moment he added, "I don't think she has enough interest in her publicity to do that either."

"Could Mrs. Farmer have sent the note?"

"Without a doubt," answered Kevin as he stuffed the last of his cookie past his lips.

I think so too, agreed Nattie silently.

Kevin suddenly began to squirm around in his seat in an effort to retrieve his phone from his back pocket. After a few manipulations with his thumb he announced, "They're skipping Harrah's Casino."

"Okay," said Nattie, "that's good."

"Why is that good?"

"Because a crowded place like that would give a stalker a great opportunity to get up close to her, and I can't assume there isn't a stalker until I know there isn't a stalker." Nattie turned off US Highway 74 onto Route 441 before continuing, "So, when we get into Cherokee let's drive by the museum. I want to think through how best to follow her around without her knowing I'm there."

"What do you mean?"

"I mean, I don't want her to know I'm following her."

"What if she thinks you're following her, but she doesn't know you're a PI?"

The road had become too windy for Nattie to glare at him for more than a moment. "What did you do?"

"I told her that you work for me."

He did not see the punch coming.

CHAPTER 10

Friday: Knox

THEY PASSED RIGHT BY THE CHEROKEE MUSEUM on their way to the Comfort Suites in Cherokee. The Farmers had picked the hotel on the basis of the positive reviews the complimentary breakfast buffet received. At seven fifteen, Nattie was the first one to enter and was promptly told she could stay and have coffee, but the buffet would not be open until seven thirty. As a PI, Nattie was always prepared for long waits. *It's the nature of the business,* she often reminded herself. Waiting was her most underdeveloped skill.

Nattie fixed herself a cup of coffee and adjourned to the atrium at the back of the dining room. She took a seat facing the dining area, positioning herself for the best view of anyone else in the space, and settled back to begin reading a new detective novel, *A Beautiful Mystery* by Louise Penny.

By seven forty-five, a dozen people had come in, so Nattie decided to fix herself an English muffin before a line formed in front of the toaster. Butter, grape jelly, a sausage patty, an unnaturally shaped square of scrambled eggs, and a banana constituted her meal. When she was finally ready to eat, she took a large bite and then quickly caught a purple drip just before it landed in her lap. The time it took to make the butter spreadable was the same time it took the grape jelly to melt enough to drip. Hunching over her paper plate she managed her second bite with less risk.

At that moment Knox entered the dining room. Her long brown hair was curly enough to need nothing more than a few shakes of her head to get rid of the flattening effect of a night in bed. Her tan skin and perfect complexion made makeup unnecessary. *She probably looks that good when she rolls out of bed,* assessed Nattie.

Nattie was not the only person to notice Knox. Most of the women took one look at her and immediately turned to see if their husbands had noticed her as well. Generally they had, which for some might have been because of her wild-child type of attractiveness, but more likely most of them were aware of her attire. She had a cute figure, but she was by no means voluptuous. She wore a white camisole and flannel sleeping pants. The camisole was barely long enough to cover her chest, and the baggy flannel pants hung well below her navel. She moved around the breakfast area as if she were unaware that anyone else was in the room.

She can't be that oblivious to the attention she's getting, thought Nattie as she watched the young woman saunter from one side of the room to the other, examining her options. Then Nattie noticed a strange phenomena: Knox made no eye contact with anyone. She seemed to look past or around the other patrons until she was faced with someone directly in her path. To these people she would hunch up her shoulders, look down, and back up to search for another path to wherever she was headed.

She's a child, Nattie finally decided.

After her careful survey of the fare, Knox fixed herself a bowl of granola and then grabbed a banana and a yogurt from the other side of the room. With her breakfast in hand, Knox came directly to the atrium. Much to Nattie's surprise she placed her things in front of the seat to Nattie's left.

"Silverware?" Knox asked, looking at Nattie out of the corner of her eye.

"By the coffee," answered Nattie, pointing.

"Do you need anything?"

"No, thanks," said Nattie, still a little dumbfounded. She definitely did not have Knox figured out.

Knox came back with a plastic knife, a plastic spoon, and a napkin. "I'm Knox," she announced as she sat down and began peeling the banana. "You're the photographer, right?"

"I'm Nattie."

"Kevin's sister?" she asked while dicing up her banana over her granola.

"Yes."

When Knox finished cutting up her banana, she placed the knife and the peel on the napkin, wiped her right hand on her pant leg, and held her hand out for Nattie to shake. "Good to meet you. Kevin said you'd be the first one up for breakfast."

"That's true, but how did you know I was who he was talking about? There are a lot of other people here."

Knox turned her head and took a slow scan of Nattie's face. "He said you'd be the pretty one reading a book."

The "pretty" compliment caught Nattie off guard, but she doubted Knox noticed her flinch. Then again, there was no telling what Knox did or did not notice. Besides, Knox had not said it like she was offering her a compliment; she said it like she was noticing the weather.

Nattie watched as Knox scooped her strawberry yogurt over the top of her bananas and granola. She stirred it carefully until it was evenly mixed, and then, after licking the spoon clean, she asked, "So, Nattie, do you like being a photographer?"

"I do. Do you like being a singer?"

"What kind of photographer are you?" Knox asked, bypassing Nattie's question.

"What kind?" repeated Nattie.

"Yeah, you know—do you do weddings, or portraits, or take nature photos like Benjamin Walls?"

Nattie's intuition told her that although Knox was described by almost everyone, including her parents, as an immature flake, there might be more substance to her than she let anyone see. She had seemingly moved obliviously around the breakfast room, and yet she not only figured out who Nattie was without tipping her awareness off in the slightest, but she also acted on her observation with confidence. Now she was asking a question about Nattie's cover. It would not do to underestimate Knox's awareness on Nattie's first day on the job.

"I'm afraid I'm not in Benjamin Walls's league," said Nattie truthfully. Benjamin Walls did panoramic nature photographs. His photos hung in galleries and museums all over the world, including the Smithsonian, and his studio was on State Street in downtown Bristol. "I primarily do assignments, like this. And I freelance some."

Knox kept her focus of attention on her breakfast as they talked. "Do you work for yourself, or does someone else give you your assignments?" she asked while concentrating on getting the exact desired tiny bite of her yogurt concoction on the end of her spoon.

"I work for myself, but I get my assignments from whomever hires me."

"Did my mother hire you for this assignment?"

"No, it was Kevin who hired me, but I'm sure whoever hired him is going to be the one who pays me."

"How much?"

Nattie had no idea of how to answer. She had no idea how much a photographer would make on an assignment like this. Furthermore, the question seemed inappropriate. On the other hand, she was sure that Knox had asked the question with a childlike curiosity. "I generally don't talk about the financial arrangements I have with one client with other clients, but if you were interested in hiring me for an assignment I'd be happy to give you an estimate."

Nattie was a tad concerned that she would put Knox off with her response, but Knox showed no sign of taking offense.

"Have you ever had an assignment to take photos at Rhythm and Roots?" inquired Knox. Rhythm and Roots was a music festival that Bristol, the birthplace of country music, hosted every September. The entire downtown area was blocked off, and musicians and vendors came from all over to participate.

"Not yet, but if I'm available this year I'm going as a freelancer. You never know when you'll get something really good or really special."

"Then you can sell it to the highest bidder, right?"

"Yes."

"What's the most special picture you've ever taken?"

I took a picture of a state senator coming out of a brothel on Bourbon Street once, reminisced Nattie before saying, "I once took a close-up of the center of a cut grapefruit and enlarged it. The colors were intense, and enlarged it looked like a part of an internal organ or something."

"I'd like to see that one." Knox asked, "Is it published anywhere?" Her eyes were squared up and fully focused on Nattie now.

The question was asked with such sincerity that Nattie hated having to lie, but lie she did. "My agent is trying to sell it as an album cover to a band out of San Francisco. I can't talk about it, but I could let you see it if you'd like." The picture she referred to was a picture given to her by Trace Noble, who actually tried to pass it off as evidence of a heart ablation. She had met Trace while investigating a case in which Frank Lester had been brutally attacked in his own carport. Trace claimed he could not have attacked Frank because on the night it occurred he was in the hospital. It would have been an easy enough task to disprove, but Kevin took one glance at the photo and realized what it was. Nattie still had the picture and used it as the basis of her lie. Trace, as it turned out, was not guilty of attacking Frank Lester. He was, however, still in prison for something else; as far as Nattie was concerned, she was free to use his picture any way she wanted.

"I would like to see it, thank you." She looked down, shy once again. "Are you going to be taking pictures of me?"

"Well, yes," answered Nattie apologetically. "You knew that though, didn't you?"

"I suppose," she agreed, her voice softer. Still looking down, "Can you do me a favor, though?"

"I'll try. What do you need?"

"I hate doing glamour shots. Can we just skip those?"

"Glamour shots?"

Knox shook her head and tossed her hair back like so many shampoo commercials, then pouted her lips and widened her eyes.

Nattie laughed. "I see what you mean. No, that studio model look isn't right for you. I think the best pictures will be of you doing something. You have such great skin and natural beauty." Nattie was going to suggest outdoor pictures but stopped herself as she noticed Knox flinching at the "natural beauty" statement. "What's the matter, Knox?"

"What do you mean?"

"I mean, when I said you were pretty, you looked like you were going to throw up."

Knox looked into Nattie's eyes once again. "Are you saying I looked like you did when I said you were the pretty one reading?"

You are definitely cleverer than you seem, my friend, mused Nattie. "You're right. I have a hard time taking compliments. I'm trying to do better, but you caught me. Still, I think it's different with me." As Nattie said this, she noticed Roberta Farmer entering the dining area.

"I agree," said Knox before Nattie could explain. Turning to see what had drawn Nattie's attention, she saw her mother making her way toward them. Turning back to Nattie she quickly said, "It is different with you. You're on the *other* side of the camera."

CHAPTER 11

Roberta Farmer Returns

"I'M GLAD YOU TWO HAVE MET," announced Roberta while she was still five feet away from the table. Her apparent obliviousness to her surroundings was as extreme as her daughter's, but with a diametrically opposite effect. While Knox's obliviousness was a facade to avoid contact with others, Roberta's was used to force contact whether it was welcome or not.

Knox focused on the remains of her breakfast, leaving Nattie to respond to her mother. None was necessary, however, as Roberta was prepared to continue the conversation unabated by a response from either of them. "What's for breakfast?" she asked as she slung her oversized purse on to the seat across from Nattie. "Anything good?" she wondered aloud, leaning over the table and inspecting what remained uneaten. "That looks good," she said, pointing at the last bite of Nattie's breakfast sandwich. "Does it come that way, or do I have to make it myself?"

"The eggs and sausages are over there," said Nattie, pointing to her left. Then pointing to the right she added, "And the English muffins and toaster are over there with the butter and jelly."

Roberta followed Nattie's finger, nodding each time she spotted what Nattie had specified. "Thank you," she said as she sat down. "I'll take care of that in a moment. Knox, is Phyllis still in bed?"

"Do you mean my grandmother?" asked Knox without looking up.

"Is your grandmother up yet?" repeated Roberta exasperatedly. To Nattie she explained, "Knox and Phyllis share a room."

I put that together myself, Nattie thought.

"She's in the shower," answered Knox. "She likes privacy in the morning."

"All us Kolache women like privacy in the morning."

Glancing at Knox, Nattie wondered if she objected to what was clearly an inaccuracy as far as it applied to her. Knox's attention was fully focused on gathering the last remnants of her yogurt concoction from the sides of her paper bowl.

"I assume Kevin gave you a rundown on our itinerary here," Roberta said to Nattie.

"The museum this morning and Sylva tonight," answered Nattie.

"Good. Here's what I was thinking: the club tonight will be dark, so I doubt we'll get very good shots there, but we'd like you to come with us anyway. That way you can get a feel for what we are all about. The museum won't take that long, so maybe we could find a good spot for some glamour shots."

Nattie caught Knox flinching out of the corner of her eye.

"We have never been able to find a photographer who could take decent glamour shots of Knox. I don't know what it is. She is so photogenic."

She sabotages them, surmised Nattie. "I think natural shots would work better for her anyway."

Nattie noticed a slight smile on Knox's face just before Knox turned away.

"Maybe so, but glamour shots are good for autographing," observed Roberta. "Don't you agree, Knox?"

As Knox stood she said, "I don't know. I'll go make you a sausage and egg English muffin."

"Thank you, dear," said Roberta. She watched until Knox was out of earshot before turning to Nattie. "I knew that would get rid of her. She hates glamour shots. I needed to give you this without her seeing."

Nattie could tell that Roberta was passing her something under the table. Reaching down, Nattie groped until she felt the folded piece of paper.

"That came in the mail yesterday. It was addressed to Knox, but I got to it before she did."

Nattie unfolded the note below the table to avoid Knox noticing. Much like the first note, it was composed of cutout letters. Pictures of Mark Andrews and Steve Stroud were placed at the top corners. The note simply read,

YOUR TIME WILL COME
IN FRONT OF AN AUDIENCE

"'In front of an audience,'" Nattie read aloud. She frowned at the page until she was sure that was all it said. "What does that mean?"

"I think it means he's going to try to kill her in front of an audience," answered Roberta. "What else could it mean?"

"It really could mean anything," answered Nattie. "It could mean exactly what it says, but I don't think we should presume honesty from a stalker."

"Of course," agreed Roberta.

"It could be that whoever sent it is just trying harder to scare her. Or it could mean that she's more at risk when she is performing."

"Or when she's not performing if he's a liar," added Roberta.

"That's right, Roberta, it could mean that, too. By the way, you keep referring to the writer as 'he.' Do you have a reason to believe this person is a man?"

Roberta scowled at Nattie. "What woman would do something like this?"

"It's more likely that this is a man, but I don't want to eliminate the possibility that it could be a woman until we know for sure it is a man."

"Of course," Roberta said again.

"I want to remind you, Roberta, that I am not here to protect Knox."

Roberta's eyes widened as her shoulders drew back.

"I don't mean that I wouldn't protect her if it came up. I just mean that I am not equipped to be a bodyguard. I don't have the staff, and I don't have the training. I am here to investigate."

Roberta's shoulders relaxed. "We understand that."

"Well," Nattie said as she lay the note on the table, "you may want to revisit your decision about letting Knox perform in front of an audience, especially if you insist on not telling her she is being threatened." Nattie leaned forward. "I also think you should hire a bodyguard. I know some policemen I could recommend, and there's an agency out of Knoxville I've heard is good."

"We aren't ready to do that yet," Roberta replied. "I'm afraid my husband is already spending more money on you than he is happy about."

"Well, maybe a bodyguard is more important than an investigator right now."

It was Roberta's turn to lean forward. "Right now we are in Cherokee, North Carolina, and whether you like it or not, you and Kevin are all the protection we have."

Check and mate, thought Nattie as she looked at Roberta.

CHAPTER 12

O'Malley's

ONE OF NATTIE'S CONCERNS ABOUT THE PHOTOGRAPHER cover story was the problem of how to look like a photographer focused on Knox while watching her audience for possible stalkers or worse. That problem solved itself quite nicely. When Knox was on stage, the pub would be too dark for good photos. That would allow Knox the freedom to watch whomever she cared to watch.

"You can do whatever you want," Mel had told her. "Knox won't notice anyway."

It was late afternoon when Nattie arrived at O'Malley's Pub & Grill in Sylva. With her were Knox, Kevin, and Roberta. Mel Farmer and Phyllis, Roberta's mother, would be joining them later in the evening when Knox would be performing. The task for Nattie at this point was to take pictures while the lighting was still good and, for her own purposes, to stake out the room to put herself in the best vantage point to watch whomever was watching Knox.

O'Malley's Pub & Grill had a small stage. The wall behind the stage was decorated with artificial stones and a large Pabst Blue Ribbon sign. It all looked rather cheesy in the brightness of daylight, but, like most taverns, darkness and a lively crowd could transform cheesy into mysterious or even classy.

"Let's mute the lights a little," said Kevin, taking charge in a way Nattie had never heard. Pointing at the stage, Kevin directed, "In dim light those stones will look like a dungeon. Let's play that up, okay, Miss Moreland?"

"No problem, Mr. Johnson," said Nattie as she thought, *Who are you trying to be, Kevin?*

"And Knox," he continued, "I'd like you to stand against the wall with your head down and your arms outstretched."

"Like her arms are in chains in the dungeon?" asked Roberta.

"Oh, yeah," answered Kevin. "I wonder if the cook or the bartender have any chains we could use."

Roberta huffed. "It doesn't matter if they have chains. Knox isn't doing that kind of photo."

They all turned at the same time to see Knox's reaction.

Knox did not appear to have heard any of the conversation. Her earphones were plugged into her iPhone. She was standing near the stage looking at the screen. Whatever she was listening to seemed to have her complete attention.

Suddenly she lifted her head and looked directly at them. "I think it might be cool to make it look like I was being held prisoner against that stone wall. What do you think, Momma?"

"I don't think that's the image we're going for, sweetheart. What do you think, Miss Moreland?"

"I think Knox has a great idea. I'll bet we can make her look like an innocent damsel in distress."

Roberta glared at Nattie while Nattie kept her attention on Knox.

Kevin walked over to the bar, where the only other person in the room was stacking clean glasses on shelves. "You wouldn't have any chains, would you?"

"Chains," repeated the barmaid, a dark-haired young woman. "What do you want chains for?" Her eyes squinted suspiciously.

"That's Knox DeVilla over there," explained Kevin. "And we

wanted to take advantage of your stone wall and take a couple of pictures like she's chained to the wall in a dungeon."

The barmaid broke into a big smile. "We can't help you with chains, but how about a big rope?"

"Do you have a big rope?"

"Nope," she grinned. "I just wondered if it would work."

The response caught Kevin off guard, which was always a joy for Nattie to see.

"I was just kidding," continued the barmaid. "We've got a good-sized rope in the back room."

Kevin followed her into a dry goods pantry and came back almost immediately with a rope as big around as a broom handle. The barmaid stayed behind in the storeroom.

As Nattie, Kevin, and Roberta huddled around the rope Kevin had laid on the stage, Knox went back to her earphones and iPhone. At this moment, a middle-aged man walked in, strolled across the room, and took a seat at the end of the bar nearest the stage.

Nattie noticed the newcomer out of the corner of her eye. He looked at home as he watched them ponder what to do next with the rope. He wore khaki pants, a white polo, and a waist-length black leather coat that was well past necessary in late April. In her mind Nattie named him "Hawk" because of his pointy nose and piercing eyes, which he kept focused on the scene around the rope.

"What are you all doing?" he asked when he finally noticed Nattie watching him.

Kevin turned with a start, "Oh, hi."

The man hopped off his barstool and, walking toward Kevin with his hand outstretched, said, "I'm Jack. Do you need some help?"

"Kevin," came the response, as he shook hands with Jack. "And that's Roberta, Natalie, and Knox."

Jack nodded toward Roberta and then Nattie before turning toward Knox, who did not look up.

"Are you the owner?" asked Roberta.

"No, but I'll see if I can find him if you want."

"Actually," Kevin cut in, "what we need is a way to make it look like Knox here is chained or roped to this wall. We want a picture that looks like she's being held in a dungeon."

With a quick glance at the rope and a scan of the club, Jack offered, "We could tie her hands with the ends of the rope and then you and I can stand on those chairs as she held her hands up against the wall like this." Jack stood against the wall demonstrating his suggestion.

As Kevin tried to visualize the shot Jack added, "You could take the picture close enough so that we'd be out of the shot. Let me show you." He walked past the closer tables to the back of the room where the chairs were wooden and more substantial. When he returned he placed one chair on either side of the stage, then stood between the chairs with his arms up to once again mimic a person chained to a stone wall.

"Oh, here," said Knox in an unusual display of impatience. She picked up one end of the rope and handed it to Jack, "Would you please hold this?"

As Jack took hold of the end of the rope, Knox climbed up on the chair with the rest of the rope.

"Like this," she said as she lifted the rope up over her head, demonstrating how the holder of the rope would be out of the picture. With her hands in the air, her waist-length shirt slid up, revealing her navel and midsection. While Kevin's and Roberta's attention was focused on Knox's hands, Jack's attention never moved higher than eye level. Neither Kevin nor Roberta noticed Jack's reaction. His eyes opened wider for a quick beat, and his slight lunge forward was nearly imperceptible. He caught himself immediately and then, just as quickly, looked at Knox and then Roberta to see if either had noticed.

Neither of them noticed the effect that Knox's bare midsection had had on Jack, but Nattie saw it. She had caught all of it and was watching him closely when he turned to face her. Their eyes stayed locked on each other until they heard a beer glass breaking behind the bar. The barmaid had returned with two trays of glasses, and one had fallen from the bottom tray as she sat them on the bar.

When Nattie looked back, Jack had left the stage and was headed out the door. She followed him out into the parking lot, but he was already out of sight.

"Who was that guy?" Nattie asked the barmaid when she came back inside.

After glancing toward the empty doorway she said, "I don't know. I thought he was with you guys."

CHAPTER 13

Friday Night

FROM HER BAR STOOL AT THE END OF THE BAR Nattie sipped on her fourth tonic with a twist of lime and surveyed the room every few minutes. The Farmer clan and Kevin had the large table directly between Nattie and the stage. It was the same table where they had enjoyed the house special, Taco Burgers, for dinner and waited for Knox's show to begin. Roberta had described what she called "the dungeon pictures" to her husband and mother.

What a surprise, thought Nattie when they both agreed with Roberta that dungeon photos were not compatible with the innocent girl-next-door image they believed Knox portrayed. Knox remained expressionless as she listened to the whole discussion and merely shrugged when asked what she thought.

Nattie grinned as she replayed the conversation in her head. She was undecided as to whether Knox was a tick, a chameleon, or a caterpillar, but had to admire Knox's strategic indifference in relation to her overbearing mother. *Why should she tell you what she thinks,* mused Nattie, *until she knows what you are going to tell her to think?*

"Whatcha drinkin'?" It was a gruff voice and surprisingly deep coming from such a thin man. He was maybe twenty-five years old. He wore a dark blue Duke T-shirt and a five-day beard.

"No thanks," said Nattie.

"Whatcha mean, 'No thanks'? I just asked whatcha drinkin'." His voice was slightly elevated, but his expression had not changed.

"Another Pabst, Skeeter?" asked the barmaid who had come to Nattie's end of the bar.

"Yeah," he answered as he slowly turned to face the barmaid.

"No problem," she told him. "You can go ahead and sit back down. We'll bring it to you."

Skeeter nodded and slowly turned away from Nattie.

"He's okay," the barmaid told her. "Singers like her just seem to get all the men worked up."

"I'm Nattie Moreland," said Nattie as she extended her hand.

"Gracie," said the barmaid as she clasped Nattie's hand.

"Can I ask you a question, Gracie?"

"Sure."

"Most of the people here are regulars, right?"

Gracie scanned the room. "I suppose so."

"Could you tell me who isn't a regular, or at least who you don't recognize from here?"

"Well, besides the table you guys have, there's that foursome in the back over there," she said pointing with her chin. "And I don't recognize that couple in the middle there," she added as her eyes moved to the right. "And that guy in the red cap in that booth over there, I don't recognize him either."

Nattie strained to see across the dark room. The booths against the far wall were all occupied by foursomes except for the one where the man wearing a faded red ball cap sat by himself. He was looking down so that the brim of his hat hid his face. Both his hands were out of sight under the table, but by the movement of his shoulders and arms she could tell he was doing something under the table.

"What is he doing over there?" said Nattie out loud.

"I don't really want to know," answered Gracie rolling her eyes and moving toward a customer at the other end of the bar.

"Oh, shit," exclaimed Nattie as the red cap lifted enough for her to recognize Jack. He had changed out of the leather jacket and added the red cap since the afternoon, but it was definitely Jack and he had definitely caught her catching him. Nattie hopped off the stool as he scrambled to rearrange himself in his booth.

She only took a moment to decide the fastest route to take to cross the crowded room, but it was a costly moment. Mel Farmer had noticed her hopping down from her perch and placed himself directly in front of her.

"What is it?" he asked as he took hold of her elbows.

"It might be him," she growled through clinched teeth. "Let me go."

Instead of letting her go he turned his head to see what she was looking at.

Nattie jerked her elbows back and circled around him. She had the whole room to cross, and Jack was already moving toward the door.

By the time she reached the sidewalk Jack was nowhere to be seen. There was nothing to do but put her hands on her hips and stomp her foot down.

As she stood there, looking at nothing, a pair of arms from behind her circled her midsection and drew her back. The move knocked her off balance for a moment, but she righted herself quickly and leaned forward as far as she could against his hold. She calmed herself and visualized the back of her head breaking Jack's nose, but before she uncoiled her attack he was ripped from behind her.

Spinning around she saw Mel Farmer scrambling on top of his captive. "I'll kill you," Mel screamed as he punched downward.

After peering over Mel's shoulder, Nattie grabbed his fist with both hands. "It's not him," she yelled.

Mel held his captive's shirt with his left hand and kept his right fist readied for another blow. "Well, who is it then?"

"That's Skeeter," she said, putting her hands on her hips again.

CHAPTER 14

Saturday:
Paul's Family Restaurant

NATTIE WAS STILL LOOKING FOR HER ROOM KEY when her phone rang. It read 2:30 a.m. when she turned it on. She did not recognize the caller's number.

"Hello."

"Ms. Moreland, this is Mel Farmer."

"Yes."

"I hope I gave you enough time to get to your room."

"Almost," she said as she opened her door.

"Well, I wanted to let you know that we need you to stay with us tomorrow, too."

"Tomorrow," she repeated. "What's going on tomorrow?"

The Farmers had originally planned on staying in Cherokee through Saturday. They were going to visit the museum and the village during the day and then go see *Unto These Hills* that evening. Knox was done performing for the weekend, and they had assumed the threat would be over.

"We're just doing the tourist stuff, but now that we know that lunatic is here, we need to take more precautions. I sure wish you had caught him tonight."

If you hadn't butted in, she pictured herself saying just before replying, "We can stay, but I want to remind you that I'm not a bodyguard."

"I know," he interrupted her in a huff. "You're a detective."

"That's right," she replied. "And I think we need to have another conversation about what you want and what I can offer."

"Okay, that sounds good to me," he said. "Knox will sleep late tomorrow, so why don't we get an early lunch?"

"What time?"

"Meet us at eleven in the lobby," he said and hung up without waiting for a response.

At precisely eleven o'clock Nattie was standing alone looking out the front doors of the lobby when a conversion van pulled into the circular drive. It drew her attention because the van had accelerated into the parking place and then its brakes were jammed. As Nattie watched the van rock back and forth from the abrupt stop, the passenger window rolled down, revealing Phyllis's smiling face.

"Where are you headed, sailor?" Phyllis chortled.

The panel door slid open before Nattie could answer. Roberta Farmer was in the backseat scooting over to make room for Nattie to get in.

Nattie had just closed the panel door but had not fully sat down before Mel stepped back on the accelerator. The forward lurch of the vehicle threw Nattie back against the seat.

"Careful, Mel," scolded Roberta. "We're not settled back here yet."

Nattie's eyes locked onto Mel's as he glanced at her in the rearview mirror. Mel looked away almost immediately, but Nattie's eyes stayed focused on the front of the van. Hanging from the mirror was a handicapped parking tag. Stapled to its bottom was a fishing license.

"She's discovered your fishing license, Mother," announced Roberta.

Phyllis turned in her seat and smiled at Nattie. "You like that?"

"I'm guessing there's a good story that goes with it," answered Nattie.

Mel's head drew back and then rolled to the left.

"Do you want me to tell her the story?" asked Roberta. Then to Nattie she added, "Mother got the form for a handicapped parking permit from her doctor, but when she went to get it they wouldn't give it to her because she only had one form of identification. Where she lives in Florida you need two forms of identification. She got mad but my sister's husband was with her, and he noticed that at that very same counter you could get a fishing license with only one ID. So he told her to get a fishing license."

"I told him I didn't want a fishing license," added Phyllis.

"But he talked her into it. And once she had the fishing license . . ."

"I had two forms of ID," interrupted Phyllis.

"And they didn't think that was fishy?" asked Nattie.

Nattie's question got neither an answer nor a laugh. *That's why you shouldn't tell jokes,* she reminded herself.

Paul's Family Restaurant was 200 yards down the street from their hotel. Mel ordered two plates of corn nuggets for the table, which were nothing like the fritters Nattie expected them to be. They were small clusters of buttered corn kernels held mysteriously together with something sweet. Both orders were gone before their lunches came. Nattie and Roberta both requested the mountain trout. Phyllis got the buffalo burger. Mel ordered the Indian Taco, which looked like the Indian Taco she had once at the Smithsonian Indian Museum in Washington, DC, while she was investigating the murder of an ETSU English professor. The fish was delicious—and clearly healthier—but once she saw the Indian Taco she knew that's what she really wanted.

"Let's talk," said Mel to Nattie as soon as their dishes were cleared.

"Yes, let's talk," agreed Roberta facing Mel.

Phyllis, who was seated to Nattie's right, leaned toward Nattie. "What the dickens are we talking about?" she asked.

"Nattie is a detective, Mother," began Roberta.

"You mean you're not a photographer?" asked Phyllis, still focusing on Nattie.

Nattie shook her head no.

"Does Kevin know?"

Phyllis's question brought another exaggerated circular movement of Mel's head as he looked away.

"Of course Kevin knows, Mother. Kevin works for Nattie."

"I'm confused," Phyllis admitted, turning toward Roberta. "Why do we need a detective?"

"We don't," said Mel in a huff. "Knox does. She's here because of Knox."

"Is Candy in trouble?" Phyllis asked Mel.

Hearing Knox's grandmother use her real name instead of her stage name brought a smile to Nattie's face.

"Candy didn't do anything wrong," explained Roberta. "She just got some threatening letters, and we wanted to be careful."

"Oh my," said Phyllis as all the muscles in her face tightened.

"Knox doesn't know any of this," added Mel, "and we want to keep it that way."

Turning to Nattie, Phyllis asked, "If Candy is in danger, shouldn't she know it?"

"That's my opinion," stated Nattie.

"That's our opinion, too," agreed Roberta, "but only if telling her would make her safer."

"If we upset her, she'll make it harder to keep her safe," added Mel.

"That's ridiculous," said Phyllis. "Candy is not the airhead you think she is, Melvin."

"That's right," Roberta said.

"And she's not the hothouse flower you think she is, either," Phyllis informed Roberta.

Roberta's mouth dropped open.

"Oh, for heaven's sake," said Mel. "Until last night we weren't even sure there really was a threat. To be honest, I thought it was either Knox sending the notes herself or it was the Volunteer."

"The Volunteer," noted Nattie as she wondered if Mel Farmer knew his daughter at all.

"Well, I guess you're convinced now," chided Roberta.

Mel turned to Nattie. "We know his name and we know what he looks like, so what do we do next? Is there a database or something you can call?"

"I'm afraid not," said Nattie.

All three of them looked at Nattie with a confused expression that said, "That's how it works on television."

Nattie explained, "For a computer search to work you have to feed it something it can recognize. If we had a full name, an address, a credit card number, a photograph, some DNA, or a fingerprint we could —"

"We could get his fingerprints from his table last night," interrupted Mel.

Nattie frowned. "That was the first thing I checked when we went back inside last night, but his glass was already soaking and his table had been wiped down. And I checked with all the people who were sitting near him to see if anyone knew him."

"And?" asked Roberta impatiently.

"And no one even noticed him, much less recognized him."

"Did he pay with a credit card?" asked Phyllis.

"That's a great question, but no, he paid with cash. The waitress told me that she had never seen him before, but that he asked a lot of questions about the bar."

"What the devil does that mean?" asked Mel as he pushed away from the table.

"I don't know," said Nattie. "It's just a puzzle piece. It might be random, but at this point we don't know what's random and what's important."

"As far as I'm concerned all we need to do is find out who Jack is," said Mel.

"First of all," Nattie explained, "we don't know if he gave us his real name. If he is indeed the stalker, then he almost certainly gave us a false name."

"*If* he is the stalker?" repeated Roberta.

"He did have a suspicious interest in Knox, but that doesn't mean he's the stalker." As she said it she knew that statement would discourage them. She knew that they had all crossed over from wishful thinking to resolution, but if Jack was not the stalker, then they were no closer to a solution than before.

"You mentioned someone called 'the Volunteer' earlier. Tell me about him," requested Nattie, trying to sound authoritative enough to move them all past their moment of setback.

Roberta scowled at Mel. "You're the one who brought him up."

Without returning his wife's look, Mel cleared his throat. "His real name is Skylar Lynch. He played guitar and sang backup for Knox."

"They were dating, too," added Roberta. "He was Knox's first real boyfriend, and Knox thought they would eventually get married."

"Did it end badly?" asked Nattie. *Scorned love would be a motive.*

"Knox's father broke it up," answered Roberta in a higher-pitched, nasally voice.

Mel glared at Roberta, who kept her eyes focused on Nattie.

The loaded silence ended when Mel said, "None of us, including her"—gesturing toward his wife—"wanted Knox to go in the direction Skylar wanted to take her. He thought of himself as a songwriter, but he wasn't. And if Knox had started doing his songs it would have ruined her."

"He is a songwriter," Roberta said, facing Mel. Then to Nattie she explained, "His songs were just not a good fit for Knox."

"He'd have ruined her if I hadn't run him off," said Mel.

"Oh, for heaven's sake, Mel. Give her a little credit. She wasn't going to let him reinvent her."

"Really?" he asked with a snarl. "What about 'Momma Zooma's Revenge'?"

"'Momma Zooma's Revenge,'" repeated Phyllis. "Is that a song?"

"It was a disaster," answered Mel quickly.

"It was a disaster," agreed Roberta in a softer tone. "I have never seen an entire audience go blank like that. It was awful. Knox just stood there, frozen. If Mel hadn't started clapping I don't know what would have happened."

An awkward smile crept across Mel's face.

"You were great that night," Roberta said to Mel.

Mel's smile twisted.

"But the next day he ran Skylar off," Roberta said to Nattie. "So now he'll forever be a lost love in Knox's heart."

"Oh, please," he said. The smile was completely gone now. "Spare me the psychological hogwash."

"How did you make him leave?" asked Phyllis.

"I just had a talk with him."

"He paid him fifteen hundred dollars," corrected Roberta.

"Do either of you think the notes could be coming from him?" asked Nattie.

"Not at all," said Roberta. "It's been a year since all that happened, and he's stayed away from her. If he was going to do something like this, wouldn't he have done it sooner?"

"Look," said Mel as he placed his palms on the table. "All this talk about Skylar is a dead end if it turns out to be this Jack guy from last night. If it's not Jack, though, then Skylar is my next best guess."

Nattie took out her moleskin notebook, and after opening it to a fresh page she wrote, "Skylar Lynch the Volunteer ('Momma Zooma's Revenge')." "Do you know where I can find him?"

Roberta shrugged. "I'm pretty sure he's working up at George & Sid's."

CHAPTER 15

Unto These Hills

AFTER SPENDING THE AFTERNOON AT THE CHEROKEE Indian Museum the entire entourage went to the evening performance of *Unto These Hills* at the outdoor theater on the hill above the museum. Knox and her family, having ordered tickets well before coming, had seats in the third row middle. Kevin and Nattie had to settle for general admission tickets, which put them thirty rows farther back.

"So how was your lunch with the folks?" asked Kevin between bites of popcorn. He liked to eat popcorn one kernel at a time. He would lean his face forward and place his tongue on a single piece. Then he would move his face back, allowing the popcorn kernel to remain suspended there at the end of his tongue for a moment before pulling it into his mouth.

"You know you look like a toad when you do that?" observed Nattie.

Kevin smiled and speared another kernel with his tongue while keeping his eyes fixed on his sister.

"Just watch the play, Toad," she told him as the first act began.

Fully daylight when the play started, it was dusk when intermission began. Nighttime would fall by the time the play came to an end.

"You never answered my question," Kevin reminded her.

"What question?" asked Nattie.

"How was your lunch with Knox's folks?"

"They gave me another lead. It's a guitar player who used to sing backup for Knox," answered Nattie. "I'll give you the details when we get back to the office. I'm going to want you to check him out."

"So we're not considering Jack a suspect anymore?"

"No, he's still a suspect. He's just not the only suspect."

"Well, then," said Kevin. "Look over there."

Nattie followed Kevin's finger to the right side of the audience.

"Isn't that Jack?" asked Kevin.

Nattie strained to see who Kevin was referring to.

"The end of that row," he said, still pointing. "In the blue shirt and sunglasses."

That made it easy for her. There was only one person still wearing sunglasses at that point in the evening. His hair was different—brushed forward maybe, she was not quite sure—and he was still too far away and turned the wrong direction for her to see clearly, but it could be Jack.

Suddenly Jack stood up and stepped out into the aisle. Nattie watched carefully as he began making his way up the center left aisle toward the bathroom concession stand area. Halfway up the aisle he took off his sunglasses.

"It is Jack," she blurted.

Throwing her bag in Kevin's lap she stood up and began making her way across the open theater toward Jack. She did not want to rush and spook him into outrunning her a third time, so she was glad for the thickness of the crowd, which slowed her down and hid her approach nicely. Her plan was to follow him until he ended up in either the men's room or at the end of the concession line and then identify herself to one of the Cherokee police in the area. They could not arrest him based on her story, but a few questions would at least rattle his cage. It might even get her his real name and address.

He reached the top of the left center aisle and turned left as she approached from the right. She was ten feet directly in back of him now. All was working according to plan until Nattie noticed Knox, who had been climbing the stairs in the far left aisle and was turning left just seven feet in front of Jack.

Realizing that he was closer to Knox than Nattie was to him quickened her heart rate and her urgency to shorten the gap between them. She began to weave her way through the crowd. Everything began to speed up. Knox was clearly headed toward the women's room now, which broke her free of most of the crowd. Seeing this hastened Jack's progress. Jack began to weave toward Knox, forcing Nattie into disregarding how upset she made people as she maneuvered around them.

"Watch it," scolded an older gentleman as Nattie bumped his arm.

In her concentration, Nattie never heard the old man. The moment the complaint was uttered was the exact moment that Jack reached forward toward Knox, who was oblivious to the drama being played out behind her. With no discernable plan of attack, Nattie simply launched herself onto Jack's back and gripped him around the neck with both her arms. Out of the corner of her eye she saw Knox disappear into the ladies' room.

Jack immediately dipped his left shoulder and spun to the right in an effort to shake her off. The move proved costly, though, as Nattie was able to use the momentum of his spin to jerk his head even farther to the right. Together they spun all the way around, landing him face down with Nattie on top still clutching his throat.

Nattie arched herself backward while maintaining the grip around his neck. To an onlooker it may have appeared that she was trying to stretch his neck. To Jack it must have felt hopeless because he had stopped struggling and was now merely pawing at her arms in an attempt to catch his breath. To the three Cherokee policemen who witnessed the scene it looked like assault.

Nattie felt something hard against her temple.

"Let . . . go . . . now," said a deep voice, slowly emphasizing each word.

Nattie held her grip and began turning toward the voice to her left.

"I am identifying myself as a police officer now. I repeat: Let . . . go . . . of him now."

Nattie pulled her right arm from underneath Jack and attempted to roll off his back. Her attempt to roll off was overridden by two pairs of hands on either side of her that lifted her by her arms and held her suspended in the air like a doll while the officer who had been holding the gun knelt down next to Jack.

Nattie did not squirm or struggle as the two men holding her lowered her enough for her toes to touch the ground. As soon as she could steady herself she tried to explain, "My name is Nattie Moreland. I'm a private investigator from Bristol, Tennessee."

"Ma'am," said the officer to her left, "are you armed?"

She turned toward the officer who asked the question. There was no humor in his eyes. She could smell the cinnamon from the toothpick he was clenching between his teeth. "Small of my back," said Nattie.

The officer to her right removed her Glock and placed it in his pocket.

"My license and identification are in my pocket," continued Nattie.

"The sergeant will get to you in a moment, ma'am, but for now, please keep still," said the officer to her left.

"And quiet," added the officer to her right.

As Nattie's interaction with the officers holding her went on, the third officer focused his attention on Jack, who was beginning to stir.

"Just lie still for a moment, sir," the officer told Jack while he holstered his gun.

Jack rolled over on his back and looked dazedly up at the officer.

He moved his head in a circle for a moment. Then his eyebrows knit together and he froze. After a moment of contemplation, he looked at the crowd gathered around him, his eyes scanning until finding Nattie, who was still trapped between two officers.

"Do you know this woman?" asked the kneeling officer.

"Not exactly," answered Jack, struggling to speak, breathe, and sit up at the same time.

"She's a PI, Jason," said the officer to Nattie's left.

Jason placed his hand on Jack's back and, without making eye contact with Nattie at all, turned to the officer who had just spoken. "I'll get to her in good time."

Turning back to Jack, Jason asked, "Do you think you could stand up, sir?"

Jack nodded yes, and with the help of Officer Jason he made it to his feet. Jason then took hold of his elbow and led him past the concession area and around to a storage room behind the bathrooms.

Without explanation, the other two officers, still with firm holds on Nattie's arms, began following Jason and Jack.

The room Nattie was taken to had a small table and two chairs. It would have looked like an interrogation room had there been a one-way mirror anywhere and had there not been stacks of concession stand supply boxes along one wall. The officers were nice enough to ask Nattie if she wanted anything to eat or drink when they left her there, but they found no humor in it when she pointed at the boxes and said she'd need an extra-large coffee to get all those cookies down.

Fifteen minutes later Sergeant Jason entered the room. If it was possible, he was even more humorless than the two officers who still had not returned with the coffee she had joked about. He was holding her PI license and her permit to carry a concealed weapon, which she had given to the other officers when they left her alone. He sat down across from her and handed them back to her.

"So, Miss Moreland, would you care to explain why you attacked one of our patrons?" His thin dark hair, dark skin, and dark eyes accentuated his chiseled features, which all magnified the intensity of his unblinking stare.

Even with the knowledge that she had a good explanation for her behavior, she still felt like a chipmunk caught in the focus of a bird of prey. These eyes were not going to miss anything.

Sergeant Jason listened intently as Nattie explained the details of the case. She told him about the first note and the second, which had come a week later. He was patient, not interrupting, but allowing her to tell it her way. It was how she would have listened, but not how she expected a man to listen.

"And now you probably want me to explain why I took Jack to the ground," she finally said.

"If you don't mind," he answered.

"The truth is," confessed Nattie, "I don't know if Jack is the stalker or not. What I do know is that this is the third time he has shown up where Knox was. Yesterday afternoon he showed up at O'Malley's in Sylva while we were doing a photo shoot. When I caught him ogling her, he got more embarrassed than he should have been and then left."

Jason nodded.

"Then he came back later when the place was dark. He wore a hat pulled down like he was covering his face and sat opposite where we were sitting. It was like he did not want to be recognized." Nattie leaned forward. "I know that's speculation on my part, but it all adds up."

"I'm still listening," he said softly.

"Well, I don't know how long he had been there, but he was settled into a booth and both his hands were under the table. There was a tablecloth so I don't know for sure what he was doing, but when he saw that I had recognized him he readjusted himself and again left in more of a rush than one would expect from an innocent man. I followed him out, but the bar was so crowded that by the time I made it to the street he was nowhere to be seen."

Nattie's pause got another nod from Jason.

"And then there's tonight. I don't know if he followed us, but it's quite a coincidence that he ended up at the same show we were attending. When he spotted Knox heading for the bathroom he followed her. I don't think he noticed me because I was sitting well behind him. Anyway, I jumped him just as he was reaching for her."

Nattie patted the table with both hands and sat back.

"That's it?" he asked.

"Yes. That's it. Now I can't prove he followed us here, but it is uncanny that he was here, don't you think?"

"Oh, he definitely came here for her," said Jason without any alteration of his face.

"I'm sorry?" she said, mouth ajar.

"He did not technically follow you here," explained Jason. "He did come here because he knew she would be here, though."

"How did he know that?"

"He read it on her Facebook page."

Part 3

ROANOKE/
FLOYDFEST

CHAPTER 16

Price's General Store

NATHAN PULLED HIS MUSTANG ALONGSIDE of the building and parked.

"Are you sure we're in the right place?" asked Nattie as she unbuckled her seatbelt.

"Absolutely," answered Nathan. "Uncle Hiram said Webb's, right?"

Nattie looked out the window at the sign hanging in front. "Yeah. He said Webb's, but the mouse with the mullet on the sign over there says this is Price's Store."

Nathan put his arm behind her and leaned toward her window. After a thorough examination of the sign he said, "Well, I don't care what Mullet Mouse says. This is Webb's."

"You're sure?"

He pointed at a silver Grand Marquis parked in the front of the building. "That's Uncle Hiram's car, isn't it?"

Nattie looked instinctively, but she had no idea of what kind of car Hiram was driving these days. She had called the powwow and invited Hiram to join them. Natalie had begun working for Hiram Moreland, Nathan's uncle, when she had left college. She started out as the receptionist, but he encouraged her to get her own PI license. "I'm not sure how you do it, but you find out more in the waiting room than I find out from the client," he had told her. And then when his heart forced him into retirement, he wanted Nattie to take over his business. He was one of three on a very exclusive list of men in her life who did not need mothering. Hiram was her mentor, and in the case of Knox DeVilla and her wacko parents, Natalie needed mentoring.

"Sure," she answered, assuming that Nathan would know. She got out of the car, and with her back to Hickory Tree Road she closed the door.

The screeching tires behind her made her bolt upright. The sound also made Nathan hurry to get out from behind the steering wheel, resulting in him stumbling to get his footing.

"Is this it?" yelled Kevin from his Honda Civic. He had been driving from the direction of Bluff City and would have driven past them if he had not seen Nattie getting out of Nathan's car. "I Mapquested Webb's, and it said it was on the right, 4.7 miles from the four-way stop sign."

Nattie looked back toward the four-way stop sign. "That seems about right to me."

"It is right," Kevin informed her. "It's exactly 4.7 miles from the four-way, but that church is on the right and this place doesn't say Webb's."

"Well, this is it," she told him. "Go park next to Nathan."

"Howdy, y'all," said the large man behind the counter when they walked in. "Make yourselves at home. Do y'all want the breakfast buffet?"

"I do," said Kevin enthusiastically. He had been behind Nathan and Nattie, but the phrase "breakfast buffet" kicked him into gear.

"Well, God bless ya," said the big man at the grill.

"What kind of eggs do you want?" asked the waitress with a grin. When they hesitated to answer, she asked, "Is this the first time for you?"

"Yes," answered Nattie.

"Over easy for both of us," answered Nathan, pointing at himself and Nattie.

"Well, help yourself to coffee over there," she said, pointing to the far wall. "I'll get your eggs right out to you." She moved farther down the counter and stopped across from where Kevin was stooped over the buffet. His plate was balanced between two of the chafing dishes full of breakfast fare, and he was tearing open some biscuits so that he could smother them with sawmill gravy. "You want any eggs, honey?" she asked him.

"No, thanks."

"Well, let me know if you change your mind." Then to all of them she added, "Mr. Moreland is over there at the big table waiting for you."

"Get the pancakes," Hiram yelled to them from the big table.

Nattie motioned for Nathan to go ahead of her, but he insisted she go first. Kevin had loaded his plate like he was afraid they would make money on him, and she assumed Nathan would do the same. Part of her wanted to eat like that also, but she resisted. On Hiram's advice she took two pancakes and a sausage patty and headed to the table. She was determined to be sensible.

"I love this place," announced Hiram once they were all settled around the table. "Since my heart attack, Marcy has me restricted to one Saturday a month." Then he winked at Nattie, "But I told her this was a special occasion."

"Oh, I'm sorry, Hiram," exclaimed Nattie. "We could have met anywhere. We didn't have to meet where you aren't supposed to go."

All three men looked up from their respective feasts and grinned.

It only took her a moment to figure out what they all knew immediately.

"You told Marcy meeting here was my idea, didn't you?" she asked.

"That's why she's a detective, folks," announced Kevin, waving his fork.

Nathan, sitting to her right, looked at her like he was trying to read whether she was mad or insulted. She smiled back at him, and they stayed like that until Hiram spoke.

"I'll fess up to Marcy if you want, Nattie."

Nattie stared blankly at him, wondering, *What would you do if I said yes to that?* She took her first bite of pancake and immediately looked down at her plate and moaned.

"I guess she likes it," noted Hiram to the other men.

"She likes it alright," agreed Nathan.

"Those are the best pancakes I've ever eaten," announced Nattie as soon as the first mouthful was down.

With a full mouth, Kevin mumbled, "They're the best pancakes in town."

Laughing, Hiram said, "They're good, but they're not the best pancakes in town." This comment drew everyone's attention. "Just wait 'til Mark brings us his special pumpkin pancakes." He winked. "Those are the best pancakes in town."

The timing of Hiram's comments could not have been choreographed any better. When he uttered the words "pumpkin pancakes," a large plate full of them descended on the middle of the table. There were about eight medium-sized pancakes spread out around the plate and covered in a generous amount of brown syrup. Nathan slid his fork under one and placed it on Nattie's plate.

Mark Price, the chef, stood behind Hiram and watched Nattie take her first bite. "Is it okay?" he asked before she swallowed.

The brown syrup was loaded with cinnamon and butter, and Nattie had to lick her lips several times before answering. "Oh my goodness. These are great. Do you do this all the time?"

"We just do the buffet on Saturday mornings, and I only do the pumpkin pancakes when I can get fresh pumpkin. So, you like them?"

Her mouth was full again, so she said yes with her thumb.

The feeding frenzy ended finally, and they all settled around the table with second cups of coffee. The men searched for bits of bacon or sausage with toothpicks while Nattie took out her moleskin notebook and set it on the table.

"Let me bring everyone up to speed," began Nattie. She started at the beginning with the deaths of Mark Andrews and Steve Stroud, the two WXBQ disc jockeys, and the threatening note sent to Knox DeVilla. She scanned over the second note and the trip to Cherokee and was just going to recap her last conversation with the Farmers when Kevin interrupted her.

"Aren't you going to tell them about Jack?"

Nattie glared at him.

"It's a good story," Kevin assured Hiram.

All eyes were on her. *Get it over with quick,* she told herself. "We ran into Jack on Friday afternoon. He showed up where Knox was doing a photo shoot, and when I caught him ogling her he got embarrassed and took off. That was strike one. Then he came back to the bar when it was dark and crowded. He was trying not to be noticed."

"How do you figure that?" asked Hiram.

"He was wearing different clothes," she explained, "and he had on a baseball cap. He hadn't worn a ball cap when it was daylight and now, after dark, he had one on. I think he was hiding his face."

"Strike two," counted Nathan.

"When I caught him doing something under the table with his hands he got embarrassed and took off again."

"Strike three," Nathan intoned again.

"Then on Saturday night we all went to the *Unto These Hills* performance, and at intermission Jack followed Knox to the bathroom."

"That's when Natalie jumped him," bragged Kevin.

Nathan looked surprised.

"It wasn't a big deal," she told him.

"It got her arrested," added Kevin cheerfully.

The tone of Kevin's comment was lost in the content. Hiram and Nathan squirmed in their respective chairs. Each gave Nattie his undivided attention.

"I did not get arrested," declared Nattie. Seeing the concerned looks on Hiram's face across from her and Nathan's face next to her she added, "I was detained. Not arrested."

The word "detained" did not change anyone's expression.

"It turns out that Jack is Jack Taggert from Kingsport. He owns a tavern—"

"One for the Road," interrupted Nathan.

"You know him?" asked Nattie.

"I've never met him, but I know who he is. As far as I've heard, One for the Road is a decent place. What was he doing in Cherokee?"

"Apparently he was scouting Knox," answered Nattie. "When I jumped on him he was reaching for Knox. I didn't know it at the time, but he was trying to pass a letter to her asking her to sing at his bar."

"You jumped on him," repeated Nathan.

She shrugged and looked down.

"Were you hurt?" asked Nathan.

"Not in the least," she answered. "It all happened so fast. I jumped on his back and flung him around. He ended up face down with me on top of him. A second later, two Cherokee cops lifted me off of him and took me to another room."

"Where they detained you," clarified Nathan.

"Yes."

"Did you hurt him?" asked Hiram.

"I don't think so," she said. "He didn't press charges."

"Is Jack still a suspect?" asked Hiram.

"I don't think so," answered Nattie. "I can't entirely rule him out, but everything he did that was suspicious has been explained."

"Oh yeah," said Nathan. "What was he doing under the table with his hands?"

"He was recording her on a little tape recorder."

CHAPTER 17

Planning for Floyd

"Has another suspect emerged?" asked Hiram.

"Well, Mr. Farmer thinks it might be a guy by the name of Skylar Lynch. He was a backup singer Knox was involved with. Her father broke them up over a year ago. Thanks to Kevin we know he works at George & Sid's over on Commonwealth Avenue."

"And I presume you'll check him out," stated Hiram.

"Of course."

"Any other leads?" Hiram asked.

"Nothing has surfaced yet. We're still pursuing the connection with the DJ murders, but beyond that we've got nothing."

Hiram leaned against the table. "You called this powwow, Nattie. What would you like from me?"

"Business advice," she answered. "What do you do with a client who won't cooperate?"

"The Farmers aren't cooperating?" asked Nathan.

"I think Knox needs a bodyguard. They hired me and I told them I'm not a bodyguard. But when I'm the only one there, I'm stuck in the bodyguard position."

"Tell them to hire a bodyguard," said Nathan.

"Tell them you'll hire a bodyguard," countered Hiram.

"I have tried to talk them into it, but they don't think it's necessary."

"Do you think it's necessary?" asked Hiram.

"Yes. At least she needs a bodyguard for her performances. The Farmers got another note this week. It said she'd die on stage."

"And they aren't taking that seriously enough to hire a bodyguard," stated Nathan.

"They aren't taking it seriously enough to tell Knox she's being threatened yet."

"Who *are* these people?" asked Hiram. His eyebrows were clinched together.

"They are a nightmare," sighed Nattie.

"It sounds like it," agreed Hiram, scooting forward. "Look, Nattie, you are the professional here. Take charge. Tell them if they want you, then they have to let you work your way or they have to find someone else."

"That's the problem," said Kevin, finally joining in the conversation. "She's not willing to force the issue like that."

Hiram looked to Nattie. He wanted an explanation, and he did not need to ask for it.

"What if I tell them that and they don't go along with it?"

"You walk away," answered Hiram.

"I can't do that," said Nattie with a slight shake of her head.

"She can't do that," agreed Nathan.

"Why not?" asked Hiram. "You're the detective. You know how you work. I'm going to have knee replacement surgery before too much longer. Can you imagine me telling Dr. Minter which knife to use or what kind of suture?"

"But I'd tell him if I was going to let him cut me open or not," she said.

"Of course. That's business. The customer decides what the job is, but the professional decides how it gets done." Hiram tapped on the table with his fingertip. "Am I wrong?"

"So what happens to this girl if I lay that out for her parents and they tell me to walk?" asked Nattie.

"That can't be your problem, Nattie," he said in a grandfatherly tone. "You are in business."

"Too late," declared Kevin, once again surprising everyone with his contribution. "It's already her problem."

All eyes remained on Kevin.

"She's not going to just walk away and leave Knox in the care of her parents," continued Kevin.

Kevin looked at Nattie, then they both turned toward Nathan. Nathan held eye contact with Nattie for a slight second before turning to look at Hiram. Nattie and Kevin followed Nathan's lead, making Hiram the center of attention. All of this took no more than a moment before it was Hiram searching Nattie's eyes.

"How can I help?" Hiram finally asked.

"I know what you'd do, but short of giving them an ultimatum, what could I do?" she asked.

"Water it down," he answered immediately. Hiram scanned their faces. Seeing no sign of recognition for his suggestion, he continued. "You want them to hire a bodyguard, right?"

Nattie nodded yes.

"And that seems too much for them, so suggest they hire protection for the evenings she is performing. Call it 'protection' instead of 'bodyguarding.' That would be a watered-down version of a bodyguard, which might be more palatable to them."

Nattie looked at Nathan, who nodded his approval.

"Where's her next performance?" asked Hiram.

"Roanoke," answered Kevin. "The same weekend as FloydFest."

"Perfect," said Hiram. "I've got a name of a guy to call up there. He's a retired cop. He's very good, and he works cheap because he only wants to do small, short-run jobs."

"Perfect," agreed Nattie. "Thanks."

"At your service, Nattie," responded Hiram with a small bow of his head. "Is there anything else I can help with?"

Nattie looked sheepishly at Nathan.

"Tell him," Nathan encouraged her, pointing diagonally across the table at his uncle.

Nattie turned her attention back to Hiram, "Ummm . . . ," she stammered.

"Oh, for heaven's sake," piped in Kevin between licks of the cinnamon butter syrup from his finger. He was cleaning the remains of the pumpkin pancake platter one fingertip at a time. "Just show him the message."

Hiram's face drew tight as he watched her fumble with her phone. He took his glasses from his shirt pocket when she slid the phone across the table. He picked up her phone and moved it back and forth like a slide trombone. When he found the right distance he read aloud, "Nice work in Cherokee, detective. I saw the whole thing. By the way, she's still next . . . and she'll be on stage."

He stared at the message on Nattie's phone for a moment before sitting it down on the table in front of him. Before looking across the table at Nattie he took off his glasses and put them back in his pocket. The deliberateness in his actions overshadowed his slowness and their undivided attention. The response they all waited for was the response each in their own way had been contemplating.

When Hiram finally lifted his head he looked directly into Nattie's eyes: "Am I to believe that this message was sent to you?"

She nodded yes tentatively.

Hiram turned his head slightly and stared at Nathan, then Kevin, then back at Nattie. "The note was sent to her," he repeated while looking at Nattie.

"Yes," agreed Nathan.

"It was," agreed Kevin.

"So now it's about you," he said. "This guy has already killed two people, has threatened another, and now he's sending his messages to you?"

"Well," Nattie pointed out, "we don't actually know it's a male."

"I don't give a shit what his gender is, Nattie. This maniac has your name and your phone number." Hiram looked at Nathan and Kevin and asked, "What are we doing about this?" His voice had a scolding edge to it.

Neither Kevin nor Nathan answered, but neither turned away from the question either.

"Apparently," said Hiram as he returned his attention to Nattie, "they want me to tell you what to do. This is simple, Nattie. And you know it is, too."

"Nothing is ever as simple as it seems," said Nattie.

"Oh, spare me the philosophical diversions. This case has crossed the line. It is time to walk away." His voice, which had been forceful and authoritative, turned softer, grandfatherly. "There are other detectives, Nattie."

"Do you mean other detectives who are men?"

Hiram pressed his lips together and turned away from Nattie to look at Nathan. Nathan looked down at his empty plate.

Hiram turned farther to look at Kevin on his left.

Kevin smiled like he was just waiting for his turn to speak. "You aren't going to win this one."

Hiram looked back at Nattie, who was watching him closely. "We don't have to make this a woman's rights' issue. Sometimes, regardless of gender, it is time to pass a case on to someone else."

"Did you ever do that?" she asked.

"Of course I did," he said. "You know very well I did."

"I know you sent a case to a detective in Minneapolis once."

"That's right," Hiram said eagerly.

"And why did you pass that case to another detective? A detective you didn't know, I might add."

102

Hiram's shoulders slumped slightly.

Nattie continued, "It wouldn't have been because it was the middle of winter in Minnesota, would it?"

Hiram sat up straighter and put his hands up in surrender. "I give up. Keep the case." Then he leaned forward and narrowed his eyes. "But if this gets any more personal, then I'm talking to your client myself." Pointing at her, "And I won't care if you think I'm a chauvinist pig."

Nattie smiled and put her hand on top of Hiram's. "At least you're a thoughtful chauvinist pig."

"So what do we do now?" asked Nathan.

"Can we get some more of those pumpkin pancakes?" Kevin asked.

"Please wait until I'm gone, Kevin. If those things are sitting here, I'm going to eat them," said Nattie.

"We still need a plan of action," Nathan stated authoritatively. "Here's what I think."

Nathan's tone surprised Nattie. At his best Nathan was thoughtful and charming, but a take-charge guy he was not. Take-charge guys were what Nattie thought she wanted. She had even dated several take-charge guys, but never twice. And she did not know why none of them ever appealed to her enough for a second round. What she had thought was a take-charge quality in Nathan before they married turned out to be an adolescent bravado he had not grown out of yet. The tone she just heard from him intrigued her.

"So tell us what you think, Nate," said Hiram.

"I still have my carry permit," began Nathan, "and it's time I got away from my bar more. The Our House is going good there, so I'm going to ride shotgun with Nattie." His voice kept that definitive tone until he turned to Nattie and asked, "Is that okay with you?"

Although she was staring right at him, it took Nattie several seconds to realize that Nathan had just asked her a question. "No, it's not alright with me. You can't neglect your work to babysit me."

"I'm not neglecting my work, Nattie. I've got it set up so that I don't have to work on weekends anymore."

"Still," she said, "there are other things for you to do."

Nathan shrugged. "There's nothing else I want to do." Then his voice grew strong again. "So I'm tagging along. It's up to you whether I'm in the car with you or in the car behind you. You decide."

"Do you actually think you could follow me if I don't want you to follow me?"

"Nope, not a chance," Nathan admitted, almost proudly.

"That doesn't matter, though," added Kevin, "because I could just tell him where you're going."

Nattie glared at Kevin, but only for a moment. Her heart was not in it.

"Protection is one thing, but investigation is another. Where does the investigation stand?" asked Hiram.

"We've got a lead on an old flame of hers that had a run-in with her father. I'll be checking him out on Monday," answered Nattie.

"And what about that message you got. Can you track that down?" Hiram asked.

"I'm on that," said Kevin. "I should know where that number came from on Monday."

"Okay," said Hiram. "We won't need protection from this guy if we find him first. Are you working on any other leads?"

"That's it for folks with grievances against Knox," Nattie said. "But Kevin is also looking into people with grudges against those two disc jockeys from WXBQ."

Hiram cleared his throat and said after looking at his watch, "Look, Nattie, you are a great detective. You get more information from folks than I ever could."

"Thanks, but—" began Nattie.

"I'm not done," interrupted Hiram. "But you have a blind spot, and we've talked about it several times when you worked for me."

104

Nattie squirmed in her seat. She knew what was coming.

"You get so fixed on what you're focused on that sometimes you miss what's coming up behind you."

She opened her mouth to defend herself, but Hiram waved his left index finger at her. "You need someone watching your back." He put his finger down and turned to Nathan. "Is there someone else who can cover her when you're tied up? Maybe someone who owes her a favor?"

"Oh yeah," said Nathan. He turned to Nattie. "What's the name of that bodyguard in Knoxville you used to send business to? Courtney something?"

"Courtney Bailey," said Nattie, "but she's in law school now."

"How about that big guy from Indiana?"

"Do you mean Dan Gross?" asked Nattie.

"Yeah, him. Didn't you do some detective work for him once?"

"He's not working anymore either," said Nattie.

"There's always John Early from Bristol or Allen Poe from Johnson City," offered Kevin.

"I don't recognize those names," said Hiram. "What's the deal with them?"

"They're both cops," explained Nattie. "John's in Afghanistan, and I don't think Allen is a good fit." She was glad no one asked her why, because the last time she had seen him was when he arrested Greg Taylor, the lawyer from her stepfather's law firm. He had asked her out, and she had turned him down. It was a decision she ruminated about for more than a year.

When she happened to make eye contact with Nathan again, he was watching her intently. Apparently he was waiting for the right moment to say what was on his mind. "You know who would come back in a heartbeat to help you out?"

"He's not really a bodyguard," countered Nattie.

"He's an ex-cop, and he'd be a great bodyguard. And you know it, Nattie," pleaded Nathan. "Besides, I already talked to him."

Nattie looked at him suspiciously. "What did Beau say?"

"He said, 'I'll drop anything and everything if Miss Nattie needs me.'"

"Did he say anything else?"

"He said he'd only come if you asked him yourself."

That's because, she remembered, *the last time I spoke to him I told him I'd have him arrested if he ever came back to Bristol.*

CHAPTER 18

Monday: George & Sid's

NATTIE HAD DRIVEN BY GEORGE & SID'S beer and wine store many times. It sat on the west side of Commonwealth Avenue just a few blocks north of State Street, so whenever she went to Alfredo's for baba ganoush or to Mountain Sports for outdoor gear she would notice it. Once she had pulled into their parking lot to call for directions to Dr. Callanan's office when she was having her eyes checked.

Not until she walked in did she remember she had been there once before. When she was in high school she found a $5 bill under the front tire of her best friend's—Shelly Black's—Volkswagen in the Science Hill parking lot. "That's lucky money," Shelly had said. "You know what we need to do with lucky money, don't you?" Nattie had no idea but went along for the ride as Shelly drove up the Bristol Highway out of Johnson City and through Bristol, Tennessee, on Volunteer Parkway, until they crossed the state line and the road became Commonwealth Avenue. Back then you could not convert lucky money into lottery tickets in Tennessee, and since it was virtually a straight shot from Science Hill to George & Sid's, that was the spot for Virginia lottery tickets. They bought five tickets and won $10, which they spent at McDonald's on the way back to Johnson City.

The long-forgotten memory came back to Nattie as she stood transfixed in the doorway. She had not thought of Shelly in years. They had been best friends in their junior year but lost touch with each other, as so many friendships between girls do, because they disagreed on the rules of conduct when boys were involved. It came down to a simple question: Are commitments to other girls still binding when a boy appears? The girls who fit in the yes camp were divided between those who tolerated the nos and those who did not. Nattie did not.

"What can we do for you, honey?" asked the redhead behind the counter facing the door.

The question brought Nattie out of her trance. "I'm sorry," she said to the woman trying to get around her in the doorway.

The woman smiled at Nattie and nodded as she circled around her and headed to the counter on the far side of the store. There, in front of a wall of cigarettes, stood a man holding out a red carton. The woman tucked the carton under her arm and put her money on the counter.

"That's my husband," said the redhead. "He knows every customer who comes in here and what they want."

"Is he George or Sid?" asked Nattie.

"That's Brian," answered the redhead with a big smile. "And I'm not George or Sid either. We bought this place in 1985 but we kept the name. You should have come by this weekend. It was a customer appreciation day for the place's twenty-seventh year. We made hot dogs and gave away prizes."

"I'm sorry I missed it," said Nattie. She handed over a business card. "I'm Nattie Moreland, and I have a few questions for you about an employee, if you don't mind."

"I'm Karen," said the woman behind the counter, holding out her hand.

Karen had a nice smile and a firm handshake, and she looked right at Nattie while they spoke. Nattie watched her as she looked down at the business card in her hand.

" 'Natasha McMorales,' " she read aloud. "You're not the Natasha that sandwich at CityMug is named after, are you?"

Nattie did not answer.

"You're blushing," observed Karen.

Nattie took a deep breath before saying, "Yes. The sandwich at CityMug is named after me. My brother did that. He's the one who came up with that name for my detective agency. And yes. I blush. I find all this attention a bit much to handle."

"It's a good sandwich."

"Thank you," said Nattie and immediately gritted her teeth together. "I mean, it is a good sandwich. I'm not responsible for it; they are. It's not even my idea. It was my brother's idea."

Karen chuckled. "Honey, you need to relax more."

"That's good advice, thank you."

"Now," said Karen, "how can I help you?"

Taking out her moleskin notebook Nattie opened it to the page she had marked with the elastic loop attached to the back cover. "I'm looking for a young man named Skylar Lynch."

"Skylar—" repeated Karen, "he hasn't worked here for four months."

"Can you tell me where I can find him? "

"I think his parents live over on Euclid. You could try there."

The Lynch family had recently retired and left town. Their home was still for sale, and the forwarding address Kevin had already tracked down was a dead end.

"Thanks," said Nattie. "I'll try that. What can you tell me about Skylar?"

"He worked for us for close to a year. He was one of the best employees we ever had. Is he in some kind of trouble?"

Nattie asked, "Was he in trouble while he worked for you?"

"Not really," said Karen, breaking eye contact.

"Not . . . really?" repeated Nattie.

Brian Self had come unnoticed to stand behind his wife. "Are you going to tell her why we let him go?" he asked.

Karen jumped slightly and looked briefly at her husband before turning to Nattie. "He was a musician. We told him he would need to work every other weekend, but by the end he wasn't able to work any."

"That's true," agreed Brian, "but she wants to know about that other thing."

Nattie watched the unspoken disagreement transpire between the spouses, wondering what it was he wanted her to know that she was reluctant to tell.

Finally Karen turned back to face Nattie again. A thin-lipped smile, narrowed eye slits, and a gentle bounce of her head to either side told Nattie that Brian had won but Karen still disagreed.

"There was this one time," began Karen, "when the cops came by. Apparently someone made a threatening phone call from our phone."

"That's why I fired him," said Brian with a single tip of his head.

Karen watched him return to the other end of the counter, then in a lower voice said, "They never told us if Skylar did it or not, so we don't know. I don't think he did it."

"But Brian does?" asked Nattie.

"Yes. Brian does."

"Who was he accused of threatening?"

"I don't know who exactly," answered Karen. "It was someone over at that radio station, WXBQ."

CHAPTER 19

Eli Not Available

NATTIE ORIGINALLY RESISTED NATHAN'S OFFER to make the Roanoke trip with her. With Hiram's retired Roanoke policeman friend, Sam Samuel, doing the bodyguard work, Nathan was unnecessary, but that was not why she balked. Eli Anderson's boarding school was near Roanoke, and she wanted to stop in and check on the fifteen-year-old. Her bond with the young man went beyond her tendency to collect stray and needy men to care for, and it went beyond the fact that Eli was in her kitchen the night Trace Noble almost killed her. The *Bristol Herald Courier* had reported that it was Eli who had saved her life that night. Nathan had no reason not to believe the *Herald Courier's* account and so had no objections to stopping at the boarding school. What Nathan did not know was that Eli was one of only four people who knew the truth about what happened that night.

Livingston Academy appeared more like one of those immaculate horse farms between Lexington and Louisville, Kentucky, with its pristine white fence, gently rolling bright green pastures, and long gravel driveway that somehow remained dust free even when vehicles drove on it. The wrought-iron sign arching over the entrance was the only indication that this was a school. The main building looked like an estate because that was, in fact, what it was. All the other buildings looked like barns and other farm-type outbuildings.

"Nattie, he's not here." Nathan repeated what the dorm mother had said.

The school sat on what was once the estate of Robert Cooper Church, the owner of a string of hotels and restaurants in New York, Philadelphia, Baltimore, and Washington, DC, in the 1940s. Church made a fortune offering simpler mid-priced options in high-priced markets. His retirement estate was just the opposite, a high-dollar lodge on a failed farmstead southeast of Roanoke, Virginia.

The lodge was now a dormitory to fifty students. The entry to the lodge looked like a hotel lobby, with upholstered furniture set up in four conversational groupings and a counter at the far end.

Behind the counter stood the dorm mother, a sixty-year-old woman named Margarette Johns. Margarette was new, replacing Andrea Jackson, who had retired. Nattie had developed a good relationship with Andrea and enjoyed some privileges normally reserved for parents or legal guardians.

Nattie had heard it the first time but could not process the information. She looked blankly at Nathan. "I e-mailed him yesterday. He said he would be here."

"I know," replied Nathan softly, "but he isn't here now."

"Do you know where he is?" Nathan asked Margarette.

"I'm sorry," said Margarette in a tone that meant anything but that she was sorry. "That's information only a parent or guardian can receive."

"Look here, ma'am," said Nattie in a tone that made Nathan shrink back slightly. "My name is Natalie Moreland. I am a private investigator from Bristol, Tennessee." Nattie placed her credentials on the counter. "I am investigating a double homicide. I came here this morning to interview Mr. Anderson. He may have important information for me, so I have had just about enough of this. I want to know where I can find Mr. Anderson right now, or I will be forced to take legal action." Placing her palms against the edge of the counter she leaned forward. "How would your board of governors feel if you got them named in a legal action in which you obstructed an investigation by a duly appointed officer of the court?"

"He's home," said Margarette as soon as Nattie quite speaking.

"When did he leave?" asked Nattie, her arms at her side.

"Seven o'clock yesterday evening."

Nattie dropped her gaze down to her credentials as she slowly folded them and put them back in her bag. Then, without looking at the woman again, she turned and headed for the door.

"I don't want any trouble," the woman called out to her.

"There won't be any trouble," Nathan told her as he hurried to catch up to Nattie.

"Was any of that legit?" Nathan asked Nattie across the top of his Mustang.

"Is any of what legit?"

"The stuff you just told that woman. Could Eli know something about the murders of those two DJs?"

"Don't be ridiculous. He was here."

"So you were just jerking her chain."

Nattie looked back toward the building. "I thought she was lying."

"Do you still think she was lying?"

"No," she said meekly as she slid into the passenger seat.

Nathan stood leaning against the car as Nattie disappeared from view. By the time he sat behind the wheel she was already buckled in and looking at her phone. He placed the key into the ignition but did not turn it.

"Are you okay?" he asked.

"I'm not sure what I am," she answered without looking at him. She put her phone away, explaining, "I thought I might have missed a text or an e-mail."

"Did you?"

"No," she said. "I don't get it. Last night he said he'd be here, and I said we were coming today."

"Maybe something happened."

She eyed him blankly. "Something probably did happen, but he went home. That means he had time to arrange the trip home, and then he had a two-hour trip. Why didn't he let me know? He knew I was coming."

"He's a kid."

That's what I need, thought Nattie. *Another man in my life with an excuse to be irresponsible.* Her eyes twitched as she looked at him.

"I guess that wasn't what you wanted to hear," he observed.

Her face softened. "No, you're right. He's a kid. But I have a right to be pissed . . . or hurt . . . or confused." She shook her head. "I don't know how I feel."

"Tell me what to do, Nattie. I want to help, but I don't know what to do."

Nattie looked back at the building. "I'll be okay," she said before turning to face him. "We don't have to be in Roanoke until late this afternoon, so here's what I want you to do. Make all the decisions between now and then."

"No problem," he said. He took out his phone, looked something up, and then typed an address into his GPS.

As they pulled out of the parking lot Nattie asked, "Where are we going?"

"It's a surprise," he said.

They drove in silence. Nattie looked out the passenger window, which she assumed Nathan would interpret as her being upset. And she was upset, but mostly she was dealing with a vivid, unwanted memory of that moment in her kitchen when her life was first in the hands of Trace Noble and then in the hands of Beau Robinette. Other than she and those two men, Eli was the only person on earth who knew what had happened that night.

Blacksnake Meadery is easy to find with directions, but it is so cloistered off the beaten track that a visitor is unlikely to stumble upon it. In fact, when Nathan turned off the road into the driveway that ran alongside the building, Nattie was startled. She would have driven right past it. They circled the rustic log cabin adorned with wildflowers and a front porch overlooking a long grassy area surrounded by trees and shrubs.

As they climbed the stairs to the front porch, a woman exited the house. She was roughly Nattie's age with square shoulders, a firm jaw, and a sprinkling of freckles across her face. "Hi, I'm Joanne Villers. Are you here for the sampling?"

For $5 they were able to sample five different meads.

"Do you ever sell larger quantities?" asked Nathan after tasting the Meloluna.

As Joanne was pouring the next sample she asked, "Do you own a wine shop or something?"

"I own a tavern in Bristol," answered Nathan.

"Really?" Joanne said as she sat the bottle down. "Which one?"

"Our House, on State Street," he answered. "Do you know Bristol?"

"I graduated from Tennessee High in '89."

While Nathan and Joanne made some arrangements about doing a tasting at his tavern, Nattie rechecked her phone for messages from Eli. Seeing none she turned her phone off and then realized she was biting her lower lip.

After loading a case of various meads in his trunk, Nathan announced, "Next stop, Foggy Ridge Cider." The Foggy Ridge apple orchard was just a few miles beyond Blacksnake Meadery. They sampled another array of alcoholic beverages, but this time it was hard cider. Although Nathan joked about having so much alcohol before lunch, Nattie did not laugh. She did not say anything because all the samples together did not amount to much more than a single beer, but the question of his commitment to sobriety was still not settled.

"Do you want anything?" Nathan asked her as he ordered three bottles of Black Pippen.

"Oh yeah," she said. When they first entered she had noticed some small bags of candy and nuts on the counter near the cash register. One of the bags held something that looked like peanut brittle with sesame seeds, but it was not there when she returned to the display.

"Do you have any more of those?" Nattie asked the cashier as she pointed at the bag of candy in the hands of a woman who had come in behind her.

"Sweet and Salty Nut Bars," said the cashier as she looked under the counter. "No, it looks like that was the last one. But you could try to get them up in Floyd. That's where we get them."

"Floyd is just up the road," Nathan told her. As he settled up with the cashier he asked, "Where in Floyd can we get them?"

"Natasha's. It's a good place to have lunch, too, if you're hungry," said the cashier.

With an oversized grin Nathan looked at Nattie and asked, "What do you think? Shall we check out Natasha's?"

They drove to the stoplight in the middle of Floyd and turned left as they were told. Natasha's Market Café was on the left at the end of an expansive front lawn.

Nathan ate an herbed egg salad sandwich with a side of "grown-up mac and cheese" with bacon. He asked what kind of beer they had, but then decided beer did not go with what he ordered. Nattie had the veggie burger with ancho sauce. For dessert they split a key lime pie.

Their only disappointment about Natasha's was hearing that the Sweet & Salty Nut Bars were only made to sell elsewhere.

On the way out of Floyd they passed a banner that read "Eat More Chocolate." When Nattie read it out loud, Nathan slowed down and found a place to turn around.

"Who knows?" Nathan said before she could object. "They may have something better than your nutty Nut Bars."

The glass cases displaying the huge variety of chocolates at Nancy's Candy Company stood as an island in the middle of the room. Nattie had seen a number of things she wanted as she circled the island, but her choice was clear as she reached the last corner where the jalapeño chocolate truffles were displayed. She ordered one for each of them.

Nattie handed Nathan his treat before he had buckled his seat belt. He held his and watched her take a bite of hers.

She closed her eyes as she moaned. Then, with a slow lick of her upper lip, she pointed at the remaining truffle in her hand and said, "That's the best chocolate I've ever eaten."

Nathan popped the entire truffle in his mouth and slid back out of his car before he could have tasted it.

She watched him go back inside. As soon as he was out of sight she checked her phone again, hoping for something from Eli. Just a few minutes later Nathan reemerged with a small box in his hand. She quickly shut off her phone and tried to disguise her disappointment at not hearing from Eli as he handed the box to her through her open window.

CHAPTER 20

Saturday: Hotel Roanoke

It was midday when they parked in front of the Hotel Roanoke, a beautiful Tudor-style hotel built by the Norfolk and Western Railway in 1892. In 1989 it was donated to Virginia Tech. The rooms are elegant, as are the formal restaurant and lounge. Original oil paintings, including one of General Robert E. Lee, adorn the lobby. Downtown Roanoke adjacent to the railway mainline is within easy walking distance via a covered walking bridge.

While Nathan went to register, Nattie stood in the middle of the lobby surveying the room. Hiram's retired Roanoke policeman friend, Sam Samuel, was to have met them in the lobby, but they were a little early so she was not sure if he would be there. To her right was a young couple having an "I don't know, what do you want to do?" conversation. The only other person in the lobby was an elderly gentleman who was watching her.

After a brief smile and a nod of acknowledgment Nattie tried not to continue eye contact with the gentleman, but he did not take the hint. He ambled over to where she stood and asked, "You look like you're looking for something. Can I help?"

"No, thanks," Nattie replied gently. "I'm here to meet someone."

"I'm someone," he replied.

Nattie smiled. "I'm here to meet a retired policeman."

"I'm a retired policeman," he informed her.

Nattie looked closer. "Sam? Sam Samuel?"

He smiled. He did not look at all like a retired policeman turned bodyguard. An off-duty department store Santa would have been her guess. He was not much taller than she, with thinning gray hair pulled back into a ponytail that just covered his collar. Wire-rimmed glasses, which he looked over rather than through when he talked to her, and the trace of a smile that made her wonder what he was thinking finished off his St. Nicholas appearance.

"It's a good disguise, isn't it?" he said.

"I'm Nattie Moreland," she said as she held out her hand.

"I know who you are. You're the daughter Hiram never had," he said. "I knew it was you when you walked in."

"So you were playing with me."

He looked away briefly as the trace smile appeared and disappeared again. A family exited the elevator, and two little boys scampered across the lobby. "I don't like kids," he said matter-of-factly.

His statement disarmed her, which he seemed to enjoy. "Your singer and her entourage checked in about half an hour ago. They're on the fifth floor."

"Wow," she said, "you're on top of this."

He shrugged. "If I stayed home, Joyce would just give me things to do. Hiram said you had a suspect."

"We do. His name is Skylar Lynch. He was involved with her a year ago, but there was a bad breakup. We aren't sure it's him, but he looks good for it."

Sam looked quietly over his glasses again.

She knew he was waiting for her to say something but was drawing a blank as to what it might be.

He broke the silence. "It would be nice if you had a picture of your suspect."

Knox was set to perform in the Pine Room from nine to eleven o'clock that night, so no one was alarmed when she opted to stay in her room rather than join in on any of the dinner plans. Knox would order a small salad from room service and get herself ready to be on stage. Sam was there, a picture of Skylar Lynch in hand, just in case.

The Farmers were driving to the Cracker Barrel on the other side of town. Nattie, Nathan, and Kevin, who had driven up with the Farmers and Knox, decided to take the walking bridge over the railroad tracks and find something in the restaurant district. They settled on Corned Beef & Company, mostly because Kevin wanted to eat on the roof.

Nattie had taken one bite of her veggie quesadilla when her phone vibrated. The text from Sam simply said, "Room 542 come now."

Nattie quickly gave Kevin her credit card with the instructions, "Settle up and come running," before she and Nathan headed back to the hotel at a pace she was not sure she could sustain.

Room 542 was open when they arrived. Nathan, with longer legs, reached the room first. When he stopped to check on her, Nattie cautioned him to stand still and be quiet with her finger. She tipped her head toward the door and listened. What they heard from the room was the muffled sound of Knox crying. Nattie held her gun at the ready and entered the room.

Knox was lying face down in the middle of a queen-sized bed. What was visible of her, from the waist up, was naked. The rest of her was under a sheet. To the left of the bed Skylar Lynch, wrapped in queen-sized blanket, sat on an upholstered desk chair. To his left and just behind him stood Sam.

When Nattie entered the room, gun drawn, with Nathan close behind sporting a gun of his own, Skylar's eyes grew big. His attempt to stand was thwarted immediately by Sam's hand, which was already resting on his shoulder.

"Easy going, sport," said Sam. "You don't want to run headlong into a beautiful woman with a gun." He winked at Nattie. "With the way you're dressed she might get the wrong idea."

"What's going on here?" asked Nattie.

"Well," said Sam, "I'm sorry my text made it sound like such an emergency. I showed that picture of Casanova here to the folks at the front desk, and they said he had just checked in to Room 720. He wasn't there when I checked, so I came down here to her room. When I got here I could hear she had," he glanced toward Knox, "a guest."

"I want to charge this old fart with breaking and entering," snapped Skylar.

The outburst got Skylar a thump behind the ear. He lurched forward, clutched at his ear, and turned to scowl at Sam.

"She's not the cop here, sonny, I am. So my advice is for you to sit there and shut up." Then to Nattie, "I think you can put your firepower away now."

Nathan, having already put his gun away, stood to the right of Skylar and looked back at Nattie. "What are we going to do about this guy?"

Nattie sighed. This was not a scenario she had anticipated. She sat on the edge of the bed facing Skylar. After pulling the sheet up to cover Knox she said, "Knox, I need to ask you some questions."

Knox twisted her head so that she could see Nattie out of one eye.

"How did he get in here?" asked Nattie.

"She called me," blurted Skylar.

His comment was rewarded with a shush and another thump behind the ear from Sam.

"Is that true, Knox?" asked Nattie. "Did you call him to come here?"

Knox nodded yes.

"We were afraid he was hurting you," Nattie explained.

Knox shook her head no.

"They seemed pretty friendly to me," added Sam.

"Friendly or not," observed Nathan, "he still might be our guy."

"That's true," agreed Nattie, "but what to do right now is the question. Is he a threat to her?"

Perking up on her elbows, Knox spoke for the first time. "He's no threat to me. I told him to meet me here. He didn't do anything wrong."

"You can't hold me here," Skylar snarled, ducking immediately away from the thump he expected.

Sam caught Nattie's eye and nodded his agreement.

Nattie squared herself up facing Skylar and leaned forward. "That may be true, Mr. Lynch. But I hardly think you are in a position to call the police. So there's the phone," she said, pointing at the desk, "and you can use it any time you want. But for now we're going to play out this little scene my way."

"Kiss my—"

Thump.

"Let me explain the choices again, Einstein," said Sam. "Call the police or follow directions."

Skylar glared back at Sam.

"I don't think he likes you," Nathan told Sam.

"I don't know why," replied Sam. "I like him fine."

Skylar, still glaring at Sam, rubbed his ear with his middle finger.

"See," said Sam. "You're expressing your true feelings quietly. I like that."

Skylar shifted in his chair. He had to rearrange the blanket to remain covered. "What makes you so sure I won't call the police?"

Stalking, harassing, and maybe even the murder of a couple of DJs, thought Nattie as she sized up Skylar's bravado. He had her, and he knew it.

Sam cleared his throat. "I wonder how lover boy here would feel about the police showing up and searching through his clothes."

Skylar flinched, and after looking briefly at Sam he turned his eyes on the leather vest draped over the back of an upholstered chair on the other side of the room. A denim work shirt lay in the middle of the floor and his pants lay in a pile next to the bed, but he did not look at either. When he looked back at Nattie she was smiling.

"Here's how this is going to go from here, Mr. Lynch." She kicked his pants over to him. "You're going to put your pants on, then your shirt, then these two gentlemen are going to escort you back to your room. You're going to wait there until I come up. I want to ask you a few questions."

By this time he had his pants on and had already shed the blanket. "Then what?" he sneered as he slid a bare foot into a boot.

"That depends on how you answer the questions," she told him.

Skylar, after putting on his shirt, stuck his chin out at Nattie. "You don't scare me," he said as he turned toward the upholstered chair.

"Leave the vest," Nattie told him.

"What for?"

"Let's call it insurance," she told him.

CHAPTER 21

Knox's Confession

"KNOX," NATTIE SAID AS SHE PATTED KNOX'S LEG, "we need to talk."

"I'll say," huffed Knox.

"So why don't you get dressed and then we can talk?"

Knox threw back the sheet and slid out of the other side of the bed from where Nattie sat. "So talk," Knox said as she began gathering her clothes.

"Wouldn't you rather get dressed first?"

"Why?" Knox asked.

Because you're naked and this isn't a locker room and we aren't thirteen, thought Nattie. "I don't know," she shrugged. "I just thought you might be more comfortable with clothes on."

Knox threw her clothes on the bed and stepped into her panties. "You know, I knew you weren't a photographer, but what the heck are you anyway?"

"I'm a private investigator," said Nattie. "How did you know I wasn't a photographer?"

Knox sat on the bed pulling on her jeans. "Do you remember when we took all those outside pictures in Cherokee?"

Nattie nodded yes.

"Well, you kept taking shots facing the sun." She turned to look at Nattie. "A photographer wouldn't do that."

"If you knew then, why did you go along with it all?"

"You've met my parents," she said as she retrieved a white blouse from the closet.

Nattie waited for more, but apparently that was all the answer she was going to get. "I don't think your friend is such a good thing for you."

"What do you know about him?" Knox stood holding her blouse in her left hand, shaking the hanger at Nattie with her right. "You work for my parents, right? They hate him. They don't know him."

"Are you sure you know him?" asked Nattie.

"He loves me."

Nattie looked down at the bed.

"You don't believe me?" demanded Knox.

"I don't know how he feels about you. And I'm certainly in no position to judge anyone else's love life, but I've got a job to do and I intend to do it right."

Knox stared at her with her hands on her hips.

"Do you know why your parents hired me?"

"I assume it's because of the notes."

"So you know about the notes."

Knox nodded yes. "You don't think Sky sent them, do you?"

"We don't know who sent the notes."

Knox folded her arms. "So, let's just say he did send those notes."

"Okay."

"Does that make him angry enough to mess with my parents, or does that make him a threat to me?"

"That makes him angry enough to mess with your parents, but does that mean he's no threat to you?"

"He is no threat to me. He loves me."

"There are some other issues that you might not know." The choice to tell Knox all she knew was more of an impulse than a strategic decision. She had always thought it wrong to keep Knox in the dark, but she was also bound to respect the wishes of her client.

"I'm listening," Knox said as she buttoned up her blouse.

"If you saw the note, then you know that it referenced the murder of the two WXBQ DJs."

Knox nodded her agreement.

"And did you know that shortly before they were killed, Skylar got in trouble with the police for making harassing phone calls to them?"

Knox curled her lip. "He never got in trouble with the police."

"Well, the police had to investigate the complaint. They traced the call to George & Sid's. It was when he was working there by himself."

Knox rolled her eyes.

"It cost him that job."

"He was leaving that job anyway. And he didn't kill those guys."

"I know you want to believe he is innocent."

"I *know* he's innocent," blurted Knox.

Nattie could tell from Knox's reaction to her that she looked skeptical, and skeptical was part of how she felt. But more than skeptical she felt compassion for Knox.

"I can prove it," stated Knox boldly. "Look at this," she said as she ushered Nattie over to the desk where her laptop was open. Knox opened her Facebook page and then linked to Skylar's page. After a brief search through his photos she stepped back and pointed at the screen. "See that?"

Nattie looked at the screen. It was a photo of a music group performing in front of a crowd of people dancing. Nattie tried but could not find Skylar in the picture. "I'm not sure what I'm looking at," confessed Nattie.

"That's a picture of Hoots & Hellmouth in Seattle. And that's the same weekend that those DJs died."

"I don't see what that proves, Knox."

"Skylar left George & Sid's because he got a job as a roadie with Hoots & Hellmouth. He was on the other side of the country."

"That picture doesn't prove anything."

Knox scrolled to the next picture, a shot of the band with Skylar clearly holding a microphone. She moved the cursor down to reveal the date.

Nattie leaned for a closer look. An altered photo that is even the slightest bit less than perfect will have gaps and shadows. Seeing none she said, "Okay, Knox. I'm convinced. He didn't do it. But what about his harassing phone calls? He might have an anger problem."

"He's a songwriter. He had given them a song, but they wouldn't put it on the air. It made him mad, and he did something stupid. He's not a threat to me."

"What do you want me to do?" asked Nattie. Watching Knox plead with her eyes was much more difficult than watching Knox's defiance.

"Let him go," she said. "I love him. Haven't you ever been in love?" Before Nattie could answer, Knox continued, "And please don't tell my parents about him being here."

"I'm not sure I can—"

Nattie's answer was interrupted by a banging on the door.

"Knox, baby, are you in there? It's me, Dad."

Knox grabbed hold of Nattie's forearm. "Please."

The door opened, and in walked Mel and then Roberta Farmer.

"Is everything okay?" asked Mel.

"Everything is fine," answered Nattie. Turning to Knox she added, "I'll leave you to finish getting ready."

As Nattie waited for the elevator she called Nathan's cell phone.

"Hi, Nattie," answered Nathan.

"Are you all still in Mr. Lynch's room?"

"Sorta," he answered weakly.

"Nathan. What's wrong?"

"Well, we got him back to his room like you said, but we let him go to the bathroom and, well, I guess that was a mistake."

CHAPTER 22

The Pine Room

NATTIE CONTINUED THE PHOTOGRAPHER CHARADE throughout Knox's three sets at the Pine Room, although the pressure to be convincing was mostly lifted now that Nattie knew that Knox knew. The fact that the Farmers were unaware of Knox's knowledge was Nattie's only motive to stay in character, requiring only an occasional click of the camera.

Nathan spent the evening shadowing Sam, listening to stories instead of picking his brain as Nattie had asked. Kevin's directions were to stay out of Sam's way, which he followed to a T. When she was not taking pictures, Nattie sat with the Farmers in their usual spot, in the front to the left of the stage.

There was not much of a crowd for Knox's first two sets. It was mostly couples coming in for an after-dinner drink or for a nightcap before retiring early. Most of these folks paid little to no attention to Knox. She was a nice soft background for most of the evening.

Holding Knox's secret from her parents gave Nattie considerable collateral with the young singer. During Knox's first break at the Pine Room Saturday night, she sat next to Nattie at the Farmers' table. Knox made several attempts to make eye contact with Nattie, which was noteworthy as it was such a shift from how it had been before. Whatever Knox wanted to say or ask got lost during the first break as her attention was drawn away from Nattie—if not by Roberta, then by Kevin.

During the second break Knox took the seat next to Nattie again.

"Come with me to the bathroom," Knox whispered to Nattie just as her parents got into an argument about whose aunt had given them a broken coffeemaker at their wedding thirty-five years before.

She's going to ask what we did with Skylar, assumed Nattie as they left the bar.

When they found themselves alone in the ladies' room Knox turned to Nattie, "You have to help me."

"What?" asked Nattie, surprised by the question.

"Tomorrow," Knox began, "I need to go to FloydFest. It will be the last day of the festival, and Alison Krause is the final show. I don't want my parents to know, but I sent her one of my tapes. She's agreed to meet with me after her show."

"That's great, Knox. Your parents would be delighted."

"That's the problem. They'd be too delighted. I need to meet with Alison by myself." Knox leaned toward Nattie without breaking eye contact.

"And you want us to take you?"

Knox leaned back on her heels and sighed, "Thanks."

"Don't thank me yet," said Nattie reflexively. "I came up in Nathan's car, and I'm not sure when he has to be back."

"But you'll ask him?" pleaded Knox.

"I guess," Nattie answered without conviction.

Knox lunged at her and, with an embrace around her neck, said, "Thanks. You're the best."

The third set drew a much larger audience as a spillover crowd from a wedding reception came en masse. It was also a much younger clientele, and they were vocal in their appreciation of Knox's music.

CHAPTER 23

Sunday: FloydFest

HAD SHE KNOWN WHAT FLOYDFEST WAS LIKE, she might not have agreed to take Knox, but what she imagined was something like Bristol's Rhythm & Roots with the downtown blocked off for the festival. It had not occurred to her that she and Nathan had driven through downtown Floyd earlier and there was no festival in sight. Rather than downtown Floyd, the site for FloydFest was several miles outside of town in the country. Other than the stream of cars ahead of them, there was no way to tell how mammoth the festival was until it came into view. The parking lot, which was once a farmer's field, was completely full, and a man in the street was waving all the cars toward overflow parking.

"Could you let me out here?" pleaded Knox. She was in the backseat with Kevin. "I'll meet you by the Alison Krause stage."

"It's okay with me," said Nattie, "as long as you stick with Kevin." She looked at Kevin, who was enthusiastically nodding yes.

Before getting out, Kevin handed Nattie two of the three e-tickets he had bought online that morning.

"You stay on her like glue," Nattie told him while he was shutting the door.

"Thank you," Kevin said just before the door latched.

Parking Lot C was several miles past the festival. It was too rocky to have been farmland but might have been a pasture at one time. They parked and then, like the sheep that may have grazed there once, they went and stood in a line and waited. It was twenty minutes before an old school bus came through and took nearly half of the line. Another half hour passed, and the same bus came back. Nattie and Nathan were among the last to board.

It was three o'clock when they finally made it inside the festival. They were told that the main stage, where Alison Krause would be performing at five o'clock, was at the other end of the grounds. As they made their way up an incline from the front gate, they passed wall-to-wall vendor tents. At the top of the incline they could look down on a stage to their left. It was Ricky Skaggs. Nathan led them to a spot out of the flow of traffic where they could watch the concert.

While Nathan enjoyed the show, Nattie took out her phone and called Kevin.

"Where are you?" asked Kevin as he answered his phone.

"We're at the back of the Ricky Skaggs concert," answered Nattie. "Where are you?"

"Turn around and look up the hill," said Kevin. "Do you see the trapeze?"

Just beyond where she was standing was a trapeze. From where she was it looked to be two or three stories high. A huge extension ladder was leaning against the left standard. On a tiny ledge atop the left standard an attendant was strapping a teenage boy into a harness.

"That looks like fun," observed Nattie. "Did you and Knox do that?"

"Well . . . I did," he replied.

"Kevin, is Knox with you?"

"Not exactly," he said.

"Stay right there," she barked. "We're on our way."

She grabbed Nathan by the arm and almost toppled him as she pulled him in the direction of the trapeze. "He's lost her," she snarled.

Until that moment she had dismissed the possibility that Knox might be in danger away from a performance, an omission that elevated her heart rate.

Kevin was standing in an open space in front of the trapeze when they turned into an area that looked like a carnival, with jugglers performing in the middle and multicolored tents dotting the perimeter. With both hands in his pocket and his slumped-over posture he could not have looked more guilty.

"What happened?" Nattie asked while she was still walking toward him.

He shrugged his shoulders without removing his hands from his pants. "I don't know. When we got up here she took one look at this and said she wanted to do it." He lifted his head to glance up at the trapeze. "It was free so we got in line. We were together." He shifted his gaze back down to his sister and then to Nathan. "She went first."

"Go on," said Nattie, trying to be more soothing.

"Then when she came down, she came over here." He pointed down. "She stood right here and watched me get strapped in. She even waved at me just before I left the platform."

"And she was gone by the time you came down," guessed Nathan.

Kevin nodded yes.

To Nattie, Nathan said, "She had this set up from the beginning."

"Maybe," said Nattie. She tapped Kevin's arm with the back of her right hand. "So what did you do when you got down?"

Kevin pointed at the attendant at the bottom of the ladder. "I asked him if he saw where she went. He didn't notice her." He turned enough to point at one of the jugglers. "He didn't notice her either. And there was a woman standing right next to her waiting for the guy who was right behind me."

"Did she see where Knox went?"

Shaking his head no, Kevin said, "She didn't notice Knox either."

"Okay," she said as she patted Kevin's chest. "You did good."

Knotting his forehead Kevin looked at her. "But nobody noticed where she went."

"I know, but that tells us she left on her own. If she had been abducted, people would have noticed." Nattie scanned the horizon. "We just have to figure out where she would have gone." Then she turned back to Kevin. "They were out of schedules when we went through. Did you get one?"

Kevin pulled some folded paper from his back pocket and handed it to her. "I printed one off this morning when I got the tickets."

On top of the pages Kevin handed her was a map of the grounds. She gave that back to him. Then she scanned the listing of artists until she found what she was looking for, "Quick," she told Kevin, "figure out which stage they are on."

While Kevin studied the map, Nathan gave Nattie one of those scrunched-up expressions that meant he was lost.

"It's Skylar. He's a roadie with a group called Hoots & Hellmouth and they are," she looked at her watch, "just finishing now."

"That way," announced Kevin, pointing to his left.

"Well, go on, Kevin," said Nathan. "Take the lead."

Kevin hesitated long enough to get an approving nod from Nattie and then trotted off in the direction he had just pointed. Kevin wove his way through the crowd as Nathan followed close behind. Nathan kept glancing back at Nattie, who was falling farther back. The crowd thinned out into another open area with food vendors on the right and an event tent on the left.

Kevin pointed at the tent. "That's where they were."

There was no music coming from the tent. And no crowd either. Nattie walked toward the tent but had to get under the shade of it to see Knox sitting all alone on a wooden folding chair. She was in the middle of the space. Her head was down, and she appeared to be oblivious to the gospel group prepping the stage for their performance.

"Wait here," Nattie told the two men standing behind her. Then she walked slowly over to where Knox was and sat in the chair next to her.

It was not apparent whether Knox had noticed Nattie's approach or presence next to her, but when Nattie placed her hand on Knox's back she barely moved. Nattie leaned forward, matching Knox's slumping posture.

"Are you okay?" asked Nattie.

Knox turned her head to face Nattie. Her eyes were red and puffy, but she was no longer crying. "I'm a fool," she said.

"Skylar?"

Knox nodded yes.

"We're all fools," said Nattie. "Sometimes we get lucky. Sometimes we don't."

Knox sat up. "He's got another girl."

"I'm sorry," said Nattie.

"She's pregnant."

They stared at each other for a moment before Nattie said, "I know you don't feel like it now, but I'd say you got lucky."

CHAPTER 24

The Ride Back to Bristol

THE FIRST HOUR OF THE DRIVE FROM ROANOKE to Bristol was spent in silence. Nattie had gotten Knox to smile a couple of times while they waited for Nathan and Kevin to come back with the car, but her mood was still subdued. Nattie let Kevin sit in the front with Nathan, and she sat in the back with Knox. The mood of the whole car remained somber until they stopped for food at a mom-and-pop place just off Interstate 81.

"How many stars?" Nattie asked Kevin as they were nearly finished with their burgers.

"Two," he answered right away.

"What does that mean?" asked Knox.

"Kevin is a bit of a food critic," answered Nattie. "Tell her about the burger scale."

"'Burger scale'?" repeated Knox.

Kevin cleared his throat.

Here comes the professorial voice, thought Nattie.

"It's basically a five-point scale," began Kevin. "One point for the quality of the meat and a second for the quantity."

"Quantity?" repeated Knox.

"Yes. For instance this burger got a point for quality but not one for quantity."

"Too thin," suggested Nathan.

"Too thin," agreed Kevin. "But too thick would be bad, too."

"So you want the Goldilocks portion," said Knox.

" 'Goldilocks'?" wondered Kevin.

"You know," said Knox. "The three bears. Not too hot, and not too cold, but—"

"Just right," said everyone at the table except Nathan.

Nice, thought Nattie, a bit surprised at Knox's literary preference.

"What else?" Knox asked Kevin, who was staring at her with his mouth open.

Try not to be so obvious, Kevin, coached Nattie silently.

Knox wiped at her mouth with her fingers. "Is there something on my face?"

It's not something on your face, reasoned Nattie. *It is your face.*

Kevin shook his head slightly. "Sorry, I spaced out there for a second. What was your question?"

"The burger scale," Knox said. "What are the other three points for?"

He held up one finger and said, "The bun. A bad bun will ruin a burger." Raising a second finger he said, "The condiments are worth a point, and the last point is the presentation."

"What about the cheese?" she asked.

"No points for cheese," said Kevin.

"That's a problem," said Knox with a well-practiced toss of her head.

Kevin laughed. "I respect your opinion, and I'm sure the cheese is very important to you." He then tipped his head and squinted his eyes like he was studying her. "I'm pegging you for a Swiss cheese person."

Knox's face lit up. "How did you know that?"

He puffed up.

Nattie grabbed Nathan's hand and squeezed it under the table.

"It's a gift," Kevin said, leaning slightly toward her. "Do you want to know why there isn't a point for cheese on a hamburger?"

"Because that would make it—" began Nathan, but he did not finish because Nattie's grip on his hand kept tightening.

"That would make it a cheeseburger," said Knox with a mock bang on her forehead with the palm of her hand.

Kevin was already in the backseat with Knox when Nattie got to the car.

"So, where are you a food critic?" Knox asked Kevin once they were headed down I-81 again.

"Well, aren't we all food critics? We all know what we like, right?"

Knox smiled. "I like humility."

Nattie could not keep herself from doing a double take and pivoting her head around to examine Knox's face. *Seriously?* She stared into the backseat so long that Nathan had to tap her on the leg and signal her to turn back around by swirling his finger around an imaginary teacup.

Rather than turn back around, Nattie decided to redirect the conversation. "So, Knox, tell us. What's your dream job?"

"Travel shows," answered Knox without deliberation.

"You know," observed Nattie, "you answered that question pretty quick."

Knox squinted at her.

"I just mean, you must have already thought about that," explained Nattie.

Knox's eyes relaxed. "Oh yeah. I watch Travel Channel all the time. I especially like shows on Italy."

"Italy," repeated Kevin. "Have you ever been?"

Knox nodded no. "I've never been anywhere outside the country. My parents are afraid I'll get kidnapped or something."

"Tell her about your book, Kevin," urged Nattie.

"You have a book?" asked Knox.

"It's not published yet," said Kevin.

It's not written yet, thought Nattie.

"It's called *A First Timer's Guide to Italy.* Most travel books are too confusing for first timers because they try to do too much. My book is simpler." He shifted into his professorial voice. "For instance, I suggest learning five words and not adding to those five until you actually use the first five first. There's no sense in trying to memorize fifty words and not being able to use any of them."

"Ooh," Knox said excitedly, "do you know anything about the Sixteenth Chapel?"

"Do you mean the one in the Vatican?" asked Kevin.

"Yeah, that's the one," she said. "Do you know what happened to the first fifteen?"

"No, I don't know what happened to the first fifteen," answered Kevin. "I'm afraid I'm not much of a theologian."

Nathan and Nattie looked at each other in the front seat with "Did you hear that, too?" expressions.

"I have been there, though," said Kevin. "It's magnificent. It's one of the things in Italy you should make sure you see."

"Tell me more," asked Knox.

"In Rome there's the Vatican, the Colosseum, the Catacombs, the Treivi Fountain, and the Pantheon. Rome has more to offer than any other city in the world."

"What about London?" asked Nattie.

"Or Paris," added Nathan.

"You could add Washington, DC, to that list, too," answered Kevin. "It's a matter of opinion, and I'd respect any of those choices, but my choice would have to be Rome."

"Your choice for what, Kevin?" asked Nattie. "Favorite city, favorite place to live, favorite place to visit?"

"City with the most must-see stuff," answered Kevin. "My favorite city would be Florence, but if I was going to live somewhere in Italy, it would be in Tuscany."

"What about Venice?" asked Nathan.

"Or Assisi," added Nattie. "The birthplace of St. Francis."

"All on the list," conceded Kevin.

"Why Florence?" asked Knox.

"Florence has its share of must-see things, too. The statue of David, the Uffizi Museum, Santa Croce, and it just feels different to me. I love the atmosphere, the history, even the food."

"Gourmet?" asked Knox.

Nattie chortled. It was a single laugh that drew all the attention in the car. "Kevin's idea of gourmet is using crushed Fritos as a garnish for salad."

"Really?" said Knox as if she had just heard something amazing.

Kevin shrugged. "I like Fritos."

"Me, too," said Knox. "I use Fritos instead of crackers in chili, and sometimes I put Fritos on peanut butter and jelly sandwiches."

"That's one of the ways I use the crumbs," said Kevin. "I also use them as a topping on mac and cheese or casseroles."

"That sounds great," said Knox.

"And sometimes," continued Kevin, "I eat the chocolate shavings off the top of French Silk pie and replace them with Frito crumbs."

Knox reached over and placed her hand on Kevin's arm, "You *are* a gourmet."

Part 4

RHYTHM & ROOTS

CHAPTER 25

Monday: Blackbird Bakery

THEY WERE SEATED BY THE RAIL IN THE BALCONY of Blackbird Bakery. Nattie had been nibbling on a lemon poppy seed muffin while she waited. The top of the muffin was nearly gone when her Monday morning breakfast buddy, Debbie, sat down across from her with a cup of coffee and a cupcake. Debbie had looked nervously toward the front door twice before sitting and then twice more before Nattie asked, "Are you okay?"

The question triggered a flinch from Debbie. "Of course," she blurted. "Why would you ask that?"

"You seem . . . I don't know . . . jumpy. Are you sure there's nothing bothering you?"

Debbie looked away. Her arms were folded on the table between them. She sat hunched forward so much that her shoulders were even with her ears. From that position, when she turned her head back to face Nattie, she had to extend her neck forward in order to make eye contact. She would have looked like a vulture if she had not also looked so fragile.

"I can't do this anymore," Debbie strained to say.

Nattie leaned forward so as not to be overheard. "You can't do what anymore?"

Debbie's eyes sharpened as she stared at Nattie.

"What is it, Deb? Are you in some kind of trouble? Tell me. Maybe I can help."

Debbie laughed, but it was not a pleasant laugh. "You really can't help with this." She forced herself to sit up straight. Then, after taking a deep breath, she said, "I can't hang out with you anymore."

The temptation to ask, "Did your mom tell you I was a bad influence?" came quickly, but Nattie managed to keep it in her head. "Why?" she asked.

"Duane wants me to be home with the kids more."

"I don't understand. We only get together two or three times a month."

"I know, but Duane says the kids are at a critical time develop - mentally."

" 'Duane says,' " repeated Nattie indignantly. "Did he study child development in dental school?"

"He's their father," defended Debbie.

"And you're their mother. What do you think?"

Debbie hesitated.

Nattie was sure Debbie was about to open up and say something.

"I have to go," Debbie finally announced. Standing up abruptly required that she bend forward and push up against the table. She inadvertently dragged her forearm over the top of her untouched cup-cake, smearing frosting down her left sleeve. Her chin quivered as she looked at her sleeve.

"Debbie," said Nattie softly.

Debbie held her hand out, stopping further conversation, and shook her head no. She made the slightest glance into Nattie's eyes before rolling her head away and briskly walking down the stairs and toward the door.

Nattie watched her exit. Debbie stopped just outside the door and glanced back to see if Nattie was still watching her. Her eyes were red.

Seeing that she was still being watched, Debbie bit her lip and hurriedly crossed Piedmont Street.

I don't know what that was, thought Nattie, *but it wasn't goodbye.*

CHAPTER 26

After FloydFest

"WHERE ARE YOU?" It was Kevin's voice on the phone.

Nattie looked at her watch. "I'm over at Blackbird. Why?"

"Well, what are you doing?"

"I was having coffee with a friend, and now I'm sending a Facebook message to Eli."

"Look, Sarge, I know you're bummed that he wasn't there this weekend, but you're going to have to let it go. You're going to want to see what I found."

"Can't you just tell me?"

"It's about those two WXBQ disc jockeys who got killed in Virginia."

"Mark Andrews and Steve Stroud?"

"Yeah, them. Well, I have been checking the Internet, and I found a couple of stories about Mark. There was a crazy lady in Asheville who stalked him and a disgruntled employee who came back to shoot him when Mark got his job, but neither of them were in this area at the time of the murder."

"What about Steve?"

"There was an old woman who called Steve every afternoon asking for the same song. She thought there was a message in it for her. Other than creeping him out with gifts she'd bring, she was no threat."

"What happened with her?"

"She got mad when he stopped playing the song." He paused before adding, "She died last year."

"So we can eliminate all of those folks as suspects. Is that what you wanted to tell me this morning?"

"Kinda makes you want to shoot me, doesn't it?"

"I do want to shoot you, but that would mean coming in, and I don't want to come in. So if you will excuse me."

Ignoring her, Kevin continued, "When my search into the past didn't pull anything up, I started looking for things that were going on at the same time—you know, coincidences."

"And."

"There was another death on the same day," he blurted.

They were both silent as his announcement sunk in. "Where?" Nattie finally asked.

"Bristol, Tennessee. That's why I missed it before. I was only looking in Virginia."

"Details," Nattie said. "I want details."

"There's not much in the paper. They didn't give a name, but it was a thirty-eight-year-old woman who was shot out at Steele Creek Park. The paper said it was a suicide."

"Anything else?"

"You have an appointment with a potential new client on Wednesday morning."

"Great."

"It's the woman's sister."

"Really? Did she say what she wanted?"

"She thinks the police got it wrong."

"I see," said Nattie, then out loud more to herself than to Kevin she said, "I'll need to get the police report on that."

"Do you want me to call John Early over at Bristol PD?"

"Thanks, Kevin, but no, I'll call him."

"I . . . uh . . . had another . . . uh . . . question," he stammered.

This can't be good, she told herself. "What is it, Kevin?"

"Well, I was wondering if there was a rule or something about me dating one of your clients?"

CHAPTER 27

Monday Afternoon

IT WAS TWELVE THIRTY WHEN NATTIE GOT TO HER OFFICE. She had a copy of the police report from the Steele Creek shooting and a salad from Manna Bagel on the passenger seat beside her.

Mel Farmer was outside her office door impatiently looking at his watch. When he recognized her, he immediately marched over to her car.

"Your door is locked," he announced in a manner that bordered on scolding.

Nattie rolled down the window of her Forester. "I suppose Kevin is getting lunch. Can I help you with something, Mr. Farmer?"

"Apparently not," he huffed. "I thought I was already paying you to help us with something."

"I can see you are upset," said Nattie as calmly as she could muster. "Would you like to come inside and talk about it?"

He continued standing too close to the car for her to open her door. "I just want to ask you a question, and I want the truth."

"Certainly."

"Did you or did you not have that Skylar Lynch bum in custody while we were in Roanoke?"

She studied his angry face for a moment before deciding to make her answers succinct. "We did."

Gritting his teeth, "And you let him go."

"He got away."

"Yeah," he snarled, "he got away. And you decided not to tell us about that."

"Well—" began Nattie, but that was as far as she got.

"And then the next day you took her to see him."

There was nothing for Nattie to say.

Placing his hands on the car door Mel Farmer leaned forward. "You're fired."

He stood back up and reached into his jacket pocket. He withdrew an envelope and held it out for her to see. It was a bill for the first month of service, including the trip to Cherokee but not the trip to Roanoke. He tossed the envelope through the window. "I'm not paying this."

Nattie sat silently watching Mel Farmer climb into his Cadillac and squeal his tires leaving her parking lot. She sat there nearly catatonic until her phone began ringing. It was the sixth ring that finally snapped her back into reality.

"Hello."

"What's up, Sis? You sound funny." It was Kevin.

"I don't feel well," she confessed. It was the truth, just not the complete truth. "I think I'm going to head on home. Are you at lunch?"

"Yeah," he answered. "I'm up at Babycakes in Abingdon."

"That's nice," she said flatly.

"It is nice," he told her. "I think you'd really like it here."

"I gotta go, Kevin."

"Nattie, Knox is with me."

Nattie did not respond.

"You never told me if it was a problem, so I thought it was okay."

"Well," she said, "it doesn't matter anymore anyway."

149

CHAPTER 28

Tuesday after FloydFest: Babycakes

"Don't you have to work?" asked Nattie when Ingrid and Lionel showed up at her office Tuesday morning declaring their intention to take her to lunch. Lionel, Nattie's stepfather, was not in the habit of missing work. Nor had he ever joined Nattie and her mother for lunch.

"I'm taking the day off," answered Lionel. "We're heading up to a new place in Abingdon. Kevin told us about it."

"We already know your schedule is open," added Ingrid, cutting off Nattie before she could dodge the invite.

Half an hour later they were at Babycakes in Abingdon. Babycakes is in what was for many years the Starving Artist restaurant building near the old train station. The sign extending from the corner of the building still heralded the former tenant. Inside the atmosphere was bright and colorful with a dozen tables and a glass display featuring cupcakes at the back. Across the top of the right wall was a wide blackboard with menu items listed in colorful chalk.

"I love this floor," announced Lionel as they entered.

Nattie looked down at the oversized wood slat flooring with good-sized gaps between the slats. It would have looked rustic if it were not so highly polished.

"Well, enjoy it here," said Ingrid, "because when I look at it, all I see is how hard it would be to keep those gaps clean."

"They seem to manage," mumbled Lionel so that only Nattie could hear.

One server—a seemingly unflappable woman named Linda, who acted as hostess, waitress, busboy, and cashier without losing her warm smile or missing a beat—managed the entire dining area. Ingrid ordered a chef's salad with the house dressing, cucumber dill. Lionel and Nattie both ordered bowls of tomato soup. Nattie added a plain bagel to hers while Lionel got the Gouda grilled-cheese sandwich with pancetta bacon.

Ingrid was the last to finish—that is to say, she was the last to stop eating. When Nattie and Lionel had each finished theirs, Ingrid still had two-thirds of hers to go.

"I'm going to need a box," Ingrid told Linda when she came by.

Much to Nattie's relief, the conversation up to that point had focused on such impersonal subjects as the weather, the scenery, the restaurant, and the menu. That changed when Lionel went to pay the bill.

"So, tell me about this Knox girl," demanded Ingrid.

"As far as I know, Mom, yesterday was their first date."

Ingrid stared silently at Nattie.

"Really, Mom, I don't know what to say. Why are you asking me anyway? Doesn't he tell you everything?"

"No, he most certainly does not tell me everything."

Right, thought Nattie, *he just tells you everything about* me.

"He did tell me he met her while working for you," continued Ingrid. "You were protecting her. Isn't that right?"

"I can't comment on something like that," said Nattie. "And if any of that is true, then Kevin has really crossed a line by telling you that."

"Oh, please," said Ingrid. "Don't be so overdramatic. He's really interested in this girl, and he gave me the details of how they met. Do you think he'd give away any confidential information that pertained to your case?"

"If he told you who one of my clients is, then that's exactly what he's doing."

"What if you were to ask Lionel for legal advice about the case? Wouldn't that make us a subcontractor or something?"

"That would make Lionel a subcontractor, not you. Besides, we didn't ask him for legal advice."

"Let's just say you did."

"But we didn't."

"Well, you could. Do you need any legal advice on this case?"

"No."

"Well, let's say you did anyway," said Ingrid. The two women stared across the table at one another as Lionel returned. "That way," continued Ingrid, "you could tell me about the girl Kevin is so gaga over."

Lionel, still standing next to the table, looked at his watch and announced, "I'm expecting a call in about ten minutes, so I'm heading back. Why don't you two finish this conversation in the car?"

As they walked to the car Lionel led the way while Ingrid followed, holding Nattie by the arm. Ingrid asked Lionel, "Could Nattie ask you a legal question?"

Lionel stopped and turned to face them. "Of course. What would you like to know?"

"I don't really have a question right now," answered Nattie while she squeezed her arm against Ingrid's hand in an attempt to express her displeasure.

Lionel took a half step closer and placed his hand on Nattie's arm. "You know you can ask me for help any time, don't you?"

Not really, thought Nattie. Her relationship with her stepfather had started badly and had grown progressively strained over the years. Even though their relationship had become more congenial, she had never considered asking him for help.

"Really," Lionel urged when he realized she was not answering. "I mean it. I want you to think of me if you ever need anything of a legal nature."

Nattie nodded yes, but she was not sure if she would ever do it.

He smiled.

As they drove out of Abingdon, Ingrid sat in the backseat with Nattie. Ingrid did most of the talking, which was fine with Nattie.

"He says they are going to write travel books and recipe books together. Do you think he'll follow through with that?"

"Hard to say," answered Nattie.

"'Hard to say' is right," laughed Ingrid. "He told me he was going to pitch a book idea to Frito-Lay: 'Gourmet Recipes for the Bottom of the Frito Bag.' Doesn't that sound just like him?"

"Hard to miss," answered Nattie.

"But Knox told him to change 'Gourmet' to 'Exotic.' Can you believe that? It sounds just like him."

"They do seem to be on the same wavelength," agreed Nattie.

"Tell her about the recipe," Lionel said from the front seat.

"They don't have a name for it yet, but they came up with this together. You mash a banana with a fork then add some peanut butter and honey to make a goo. Then guess what you add."

"Frito crumbs," blurted Lionel. "I tried it myself last night. It was delicious."

Nattie stared at the back of Lionel's head in disbelief. When she was in high school, Nattie firmly believed that Lionel O'Brien was the stiffest man who ever lived. The idea that he would actually add Frito crumbs to Kevin's goo and eat it simply did not compute. Then she looked at Ingrid, who was watching her with a big grin. As if to say, "It's true," she nodded her head at what Nattie assumed was a look of befuddlement on her face.

Lionel's phone rang. He cleared his throat before answering. "Yes, this is Lionel O'Brien."

Pause.

"Thank you for returning my call, Mr. Farmer."

Hearing Mr. Farmer's name triggered a flinch of Nattie's eyebrows, which Ingrid immediately followed by taking Natalie's hand and squeezing it.

"I am with the law firm of O'Brien and Associates out of Johnson City, and I am calling on behalf of the Natasha McMorales Detective Agency."

This caused Nattie to scoot forward on her seat in an attempt to get closer to the phone in Lionel's ear.

Ingrid tugged at Nattie's hand, and when she got her attention Ingrid put her finger across her lips and slowly shook her head no.

"I understand you have terminated your contract with Ms. Moreland."

Pause.

"Yes, Mr. Farmer, you certainly have the right to do that. What you do not have the right to do is refuse to pay for services already rendered."

Pause.

"Oh, yes, that is true. If you had a contract that guaranteed specific results, then the contract would not have been met unless the results were met. But that is not relevant here. Your contract is for specific services, and the only grounds for refusing to pay are if those services were not met. And that, sir, is not the case."

Pause.

"Well, you are welcome to try that, Mr. Farmer, but before you do I strongly suggest you talk to your own attorney, because if we settle this in court we won't be collecting just what you owe Ms. Moreland. We will be collecting all the attorney fees incurred while collecting this debt. You might also want to do some background checks on my law firm. We enjoy a fairly well-established reputation as litigators, and I can guarantee you this: If we have to go to court, I will bring the full resources of my firm to the case. And if we win—and I can assure you we *will* win—then this will be much more expensive."

Pause.

"That's good, Mr. Farmer. I think talking to your lawyer is exactly what you should do. And in the interest of full disclosure, I feel it is necessary to tell you that my zeal in seeing this through is not because Ms. Moreland is a client. It's because she's my daughter."

CHAPTER 29

Wednesday Morning: The Sister

NATTIE ASSUMED THAT THE WOMAN WHO JUST WALKED into her office was her ten o'clock appointment, Stacy Renee, the sister of Susan Renee, the social worker who committed suicide in Steele Creek Park. The woman was about five-feet-nine, athletic build, brown hair, fair skin, and blue eyes that sparkled. Stacy, if indeed it was Stacy, flashed Nattie a big smile but said nothing. She was obviously listening to someone or something on the cell phone she held to her ear.

"Listen, D'Andre, I'm here in the detective's office, so I have to go now. You're his father. You can handle this." With that she took the phone away from her ear and pushed a button. "Let me turn this off." Then, reaching across Nattie's desk, she extended her hand. "I'm Stacy Renee. Natasha McMorales, I presume?"

Ugh, Kevin, thought Nattie. The Natasha McMorales name Kevin had given her when she started her own agency had marginal usefulness for her very first client, but now it was more of a nuisance she tolerated because. . . . Well, she had no idea why she tolerated it. Maybe it was something that did not bother her until it bothered her.

"Nattie. Nattie Moreland," said Nattie as she clasped Stacy's hand.

Stacy nodded and sat down. "Sorry about the phone. I left two kids

156

at home with their father. He's actually a really good dad, but our two-year-old really gives him a run for his money when it's time to get dressed and go to Grandma's. Do you have kids?"

"No."

Pointing over her shoulder toward State Street, Stacy said, "Hey, the downtown area here is looking very nice."

"Thank you," said Nattie.

"I was here about fifteen years ago. I went to King College. Or is it 'university' now? Played basketball. Majored in coaching."

"That's great," said Nattie. "You look like you could still play."

Stacy shrugged and looked a little embarrassed. "Thanks. My kids keep me going."

"Where do you live now?"

"Haymarket, Virginia. It's about five and a half hours up 81. Just west of DC. I came down last night and spent the night in Wise, where my brother Ryan lives. He and his wife, Heidi, both went to King, too. Heidi and I came down this morning looking for a place to have coffee."

"We've got no shortage of that," observed Nattie.

Stacy squirmed to the edge of her seat. "Well, like I said, I have two kids, so I'm hoping we can take care of this with one visit. I have to get back to Haymarket this afternoon, so I sure hope you can help me."

"I'll do my best," said Nattie. "What is it that you want me to do?"

Stacy opened her handbag and withdrew a piece of paper, which she handed to Nattie. It was a copy of the *Bristol Herald Courier*'s account of Susan Renee's death. "I assume you know that Susan is my sister and this is why I'm here."

"Yes," answered Nattie. "Kevin—that's who you talked to on Mon - day—told me you don't agree with the police report."

"That's correct. They designated it a suicide."

"And you don't think it was a suicide."

"Absolutely not," answered Stacy emphatically.

Nattie studied Stacy's face. Her eyes narrowed as her jaw flinched. Clearly this woman believed that her sister's death was not a suicide. It was not a moment Nattie had faced before, but it was one she had anticipated with dread. Most of the time, survivors of suicide victims want it to be untrue. It was a natural part of the grieving process. The last thing Nattie wanted to do was take advantage of someone's grief. Another last thing she did not want to do was step on anyone's last remnant of hope. *Tread softly,* she reminded herself.

"Look," continued Stacy, "I know the police believe I'm just a sister who isn't letting go, but you have to believe me. My sister would not have committed suicide."

"Do you have a reason to believe the police missed something in their investigation?" asked Nattie in as gentle a voice as she could muster.

"Absolutely," said Stacy as she slid to the edge of her chair. "Do you know who Mark Andrews is?"

Nattie held her poker face. She preferred to listen rather than speak when she was still unsure about her client's agenda. "I'm not sure. Why don't you refresh my memory."

"He is—I mean, he was—a DJ over at WXBQ."

"Of course," blurted Nattie as she recognized the name associated with the Knox DeVilla case. "He and his partner, Steve Stroud, were murdered."

"On the same day that Susan died," asserted Stacy. "Susan was in love with him. I talked to her the day before she died, and she said their relationship was about to turn a corner."

"'About to turn a corner,'" repeated Nattie. "What does that mean?"

Stacy frowned. "I don't know specifically what it means. I wish I did, but for sure it meant their relationship was about to get better.

She was happy. I mean really happy. I even said, 'You sound happy' to her, and she said, 'I am.' Who does that right before committing suicide?"

Nattie remembered from a psychology class that sometimes depressed people have a sudden elation after they decide to commit suicide, but Nattie felt that relating such information would be inappropriate. "Was Susan depressed before that?" asked Nattie.

"Not at all. She loved her work, and she had some good friends."

"Isn't it possible that finding out her new boyfriend was killed put her into a state of despair?"

"Yes, absolutely. And that's what I thought until I got the contents of her purse last week. She was wearing Baby Rose."

"Lipstick?" clarified Nattie.

"Yes, lipstick. If she left the house wearing Baby Rose, I guarantee she was planning on meeting a man."

CHAPTER 30

Wednesday Afternoon: A Working Lunch

"DID YOU TAKE THE CASE?" ASKED KEVIN as he looked at Nattie watching Stacy drive from the parking lot outside their office.

"I did," she said, wondering to herself if a male detective would have bought that a particular shade of lipstick was strong enough evidence to rule out suicide. "I don't have any more appointments today, do I?"

"Nope."

"Good. Keep it that way. I think I'm going to be reading all afternoon." Turning away from the window she asked, "Do you still have that report from Bristol, Virginia, PD?"

"The report about the two DJs?"

"Yes."

"I'll look," Kevin said, gritting his teeth, "but I don't think I kept it." Then holding his hands up in surrender he added, "If I don't have it, I can get another right away. We already got approval to have it."

Nattie nodded and headed back into her office. She settled behind her desk and searched through her bag for the Bristol, Tennessee, PD report on Susan Renee's death. Before she found it her phone rang.

"Hello."

"Hey, Nattie. What are you doing?" It was Nathan.

"I'm probably going to get takeout and eat in. I just got a new case, and there's a lot of reading I need to do to get started."

"Buy me lunch and I'll help."

"Shouldn't you be working this afternoon?"

"Everything here is under control. I'm heading over now. Need anything?"

"Wait a minute," she said before putting her hand over her phone. "Kevin," she called out.

Kevin appeared in her doorway.

"Did you find that report yet?" she asked.

"Nope," answered Kevin. "But I called them already. They're getting another copy ready for us now."

"Thanks," she said to Kevin. Then taking her hand off her phone she told Nathan, "If you don't mind, you could pick up a report for me over at the Bristol, Virginia, police station."

"I'm on the way."

After hanging up the phone Nattie once again called out, "Kevin."

When he reappeared in the doorway she told him, "Take some money from petty cash and go get lunch for you and Nathan and me."

"What do you want?" he asked.

"You decide," she told him.

He flashed the okay sign with his hand before turning away.

For the next twenty minutes Nattie used her solitude to do a superficial reread of the report on Susan Renee. The most salient justification for the determination of death by suicide was the presence of a Smith and Weston .38 with her fingerprints on it.

She was making a fresh pot of decaf coffee when Nathan opened the front door, letting Kevin enter first. Kevin cradled a large paper bag in his left arm and toted a smaller bag in his right hand. "I hope you're hungry," he announced.

Kevin began unpacking his bags on Nattie's desk while she fetched paper plates, napkins, and bottles of water from the hospitality area behind Kevin's desk. "Do we need forks?" she yelled.

"Yes, and extra napkins. It's barbecue."

"Where is it from?" asked Nathan as he followed Nattie into her office.

"Bristol BBQ on Volunteer. I got the family pack. Pulled pork and buns for four sandwiches and three sides."

Nathan took the top off of the container closest to him. "Macaroni and cheese," he announced.

"Cole slaw and baked beans," said Kevin, pointing at the other two containers.

Nattie went first, taking a small amount from each container but not a bun.

Nathan made himself a sandwich and took healthy portions of beans and macaroni and cheese.

Kevin made two sandwiches for himself. One he topped with coleslaw, the other with baked beans.

With the exception of several "ummms," they ate in silence until Kevin moaned, "Oh, man." A portion of the contents of the pork and baked beans sandwich had escaped the bun and landed in his lap.

"What's happening with Knox?" asked Nathan when the feasting slowed down.

"Do you want my answer or Kevin's?" answered Nattie.

Nathan looked at Kevin just as Kevin was scraping the spill from his pants with a fork. "We're dating," he said as he popped the glop in his mouth. He smiled proudly.

"I'm happy for you, man, but I can't say I'm surprised," Nathan told him. To Nattie he asked, "And what's your answer?"

"Do you remember that Skylar kid we caught and lost in Roanoke?" began Nattie. "Well, that, and then the fiasco at FloydFest got us fired."

Nathan scrunched his face. "Really?"

"Yeah, really," said Nattie. "Knox's father was really upset."

"Yeah," added Kevin, "and he threatened to stiff her, too."

"Can he do that?" asked Nathan.

"He can try, but if he does he's going to have to duke it out with Lionel in court," boasted Kevin.

Nathan looked to Nattie for an explanation. He knew how strained Nattie's relationship with her stepfather was.

"Knox's father told me he wasn't going to pay on Monday. Yesterday Mom and Lionel took me out to lunch, and they timed it so I'd hear him threaten Mr. Farmer over the phone."

"Wow," was Nathan's response.

"Yeah, wow," agreed Nattie. "It was impressive." A gentle smile crept across her face. "It was really sweet."

After a respectful silence Nattie stood up and said, "Time for work, gentlemen."

With that, Nattie began putting the lids back on the containers of food while Kevin collected the garbage.

"What do you want me to do?" asked Nathan.

"You could get us coffee if you want."

Once the remains of lunch were removed, Nattie settled behind her desk to study the Bristol, Virginia, PD's report on the murders of Mark Andrews and Steve Stroud. Nathan sat across from her, doing the same with the Bristol, Tennessee, report on the death of Susan Renee. Kevin was behind the computer at his desk looking for information on Susan Renee.

Two hours and several interruptions later, the pot of coffee was empty and they reconvened to compare notes.

"What was the estimated time of death for Susan Renee?" asked Nattie.

"Between five and six o'clock," answered Nathan after flipping through a couple of pages.

"Then that means she could not have known Mark Andrews was

dead because they weren't discovered until seven thirty that night," said Nattie.

"She couldn't have known unless she was there herself," observed Nathan. "What was the caliber of the bullets?"

"The same as with her: thirty-eight. But both men were killed with single shots to the forehead. That's not rage or passion. That's an assassination. We can check on it, but I seriously doubt she had that kind of skill. What did you discover?"

Nathan flipped the file onto her desk. "There's nothing really to note about what is there. I think they called it a suicide because there wasn't a reason to call it anything else. It is curious, though, that there's no ballistics report."

Nattie picked up the report. "Nice catch, Nate. I'm sure they still have that weapon. I'll be requesting a ballistics test." She turned her attention toward Kevin.

"There's not much out there on her," began Kevin. "You already know about her family. She got an MSW from Radford, and she'd worked at Southwest Virginia Social Services for the last nine years. I'm still working on her financials. What about you?"

"I think I'll pay a call on her boss."

CHAPTER 31

Friday: Social Services of Southwest Virginia

"YOU'LL HAVE TO FORGIVE ME," ESTHER SAID. "They made this appointment for me while I was out of the country."

"That's okay," Nattie said. "It was just Wednesday afternoon when I called to make an appointment with you. They told me you were speaking in Albania. Is that right?"

"Yes. I was at a girls' home in Albania called Eagles' Wings."

"What did you speak on?"

"Trauma care."

"Is that your specialty?"

"Specialty?"

Nattie flinched. "I'm sorry. Is that not the right word?"

Esther grinned. Clearly she had noticed Nattie's discomfort. Rather than feeling mocked by the grin, Nattie felt identified with. It was reassuring.

"Do you mean to ask what my therapy specialty is?"

"Yes."

"We don't really specialize here, but if we did I suppose mine would be grief counseling and working with trauma-marginalized women and kiddos. Are you looking for something in particular?"

"Not exactly. Well, I mean, sort of," she exhaled loudly.

"Slow down," encouraged Esther.

Nattie handed her a card. "I should have introduced myself right away. I'm Nattie Moreland. I'm a private investigator from Bristol."

"I see that," said Esther.

Nattie waited for the proverbial question about the name Natasha.

Instead Esther stood up, circled her desk, and extended her hand. "Hi, Nattie. I'm Esther. What can I do for you?"

"Aren't you going to ask me about that name?"

Esther shrugged. "Do you mean the name of your agency?"

"Yes. Most people get thrown by that name. You wouldn't believe how often I have to explain that I'm not Natasha."

Esther sat back on the edge of her desk and studied the card. "I don't know why. The big words in the middle of a business card are usually the name of the business, and the smaller name at the bottom is usually a person, isn't it?"

"Yes."

"Well," said Esther as she placed the card on the desk behind her, "it is a great name and I'll surely remember it, but what it means seems perfectly clear to me. So, what does a private detective want with us?"

"I'm investigating the death of Susan Renee."

The pleasant, playful expression left Esther's face and was replaced with a more somber one. She nodded and circled back to the chair behind her desk.

Nattie waited.

"Susan and I worked together. I was her supervisor on paper, but she didn't need any supervision. In fact, she did as much mentoring of younger staff as I did. She is sorely missed." Esther paused and stared at her hands folded on top of the desk. When she looked up, in a weak voice she said, "We were told it was a suicide."

"That was—I mean, that still is—the official designation, but some evidence has come forward that justifies reopening the investigation."

"Are you at liberty to say what that is?"

"Not really," answered Nattie apologetically.

Lifting her hands palms forward, Esther said, "I'm sorry. I shouldn't have asked that."

"No, that's okay. I just can't talk about that now. But if you want I can give you more details when this gets settled."

"I do understand, really. I'm just a little anxious about this. I didn't want to believe it was a suicide, but that could be because I really didn't believe it—but it could also be a way to manage my own guilt."

"Your guilt?"

Esther shrugged. "I don't care who you are. If a friend of yours commits suicide, you are going to rethink every interaction you ever had, looking for something you did wrong or something you could have done better. It's very hard not to wonder what you did wrong. And the sad thing is that you can never, ever answer those questions."

"Well, let me say this," began Nattie. "The evidence we found is real, and beyond that, we found something missing from the police report."

Esther tipped her head toward Nattie and again asked, "How can I help?"

"I'm looking for information. Is there anything you can tell me about Susan that might help me understand her?"

"I'd say everyone who worked here thought of her as a big sister."

"So, no conflicts with coworkers?" stated Nattie.

"None."

"How about clients? Was she working with someone who might have had a grudge?"

"No. She mostly worked with at-risk kids," said Esther. Then her eyes seemed to drift off to her right.

Nattie held her tongue until Esther's eyes reengaged her.

"I can't tell you any details, but there was one young woman Susie worked with who was particularly curious about her death. I mean, she called every other day for a while asking for details."

Nattie leaned forward. "I know you have confidentiality concerns, but it would really help if I could talk to this woman."

"You know I can't tell you anything without her permission."

"But if she gives permission?"

"If she okays it, I'll give her your number. Fair enough?"

"Fair enough," repeated Nattie. "Thanks."

Standing up, Esther said, "I hope that works out for you. But now I need to get ready for a staff meeting."

Esther walked her to the door and stopped. "I'm sorry I unloaded on you. You were probably thinking that we counselor types are guilt proof."

"Not at all," said Nattie, touching her elbow. "You counselor types are probably more in touch with your guilt than the rest of us."

Esther laughed. "We are indeed, Natasha."

CHAPTER 32

Saturday Evening: Date with Nathan

"How did you hear about this place?" asked Nattie as they drove through Damascus. All Nathan had told her was that it was out of town.

"Talk at the bar," answered Nathan. "The third time I heard it made me curious enough to check it out online. It seemed like a place you'd really like."

"Did you check it out yourself first?"

"Ahhhh," he stammered.

"I'm kidding," she told him as she stroked his right arm. "Does it ruin the surprise if you tell me how much farther we have to go?"

"No. Does it ruin your evening if I don't?"

"Are you saying I've got a control issue?"

"Ahhhh," he stammered again.

She tipped her head back and laughed. "This just keeps getting easier."

"What?"

"Making you say, 'Ahhhh.'"

"Ahhhh," he said without stammering.

"Besides," she continued, "of course I have control issues. I know it. You know it. We've even talked about it."

He nodded. "So, do you still want me to tell you how much farther?"

"Nope," she answered. "I'm going to let you do it however you want to do it. It's your idea, and I'm going to let it be yours."

Twenty minutes later they were most of the way through Mountain City. That's when Nathan slowed down and turned into a parking lot on the right. "Subas" read the sign.

"I'm Ryne Sandberg," said Nathan to the hostess, a buxom forty-something woman with a toothy smile and enough freckles for a kindergarten class.

"We have you all set, Mr. Sandberg. Follow me," said the very cheerful hostess.

Before letting her follow the hostess, Nathan glanced at Nattie to see if she was smiling. She was. Ryne Sandberg was her grandfather's favorite Chicago Cub. Whenever the Wolf, Nattie's grandfather, left his name in a restaurant, he used Ryne Sandberg's name. The attention that received in the Chicago area twenty years earlier was significantly more than it did right then in Mountain City, where it went unnoticed. But Nattie noticed, and that was all that mattered.

After they were seated against the back wall, the hostess handed them menus and asked, "Can I take your drink orders?"

"We don't need menus," Nathan informed her. "I ordered ahead."

"You did?" responded a slightly startled Nattie. This much take-charge was not Nathan's usual operating procedure.

"I did," he said with pronounced satisfaction. Then, turning to the hostess, he said, "She's going to want to read the whole menu."

"That's okay," said the hostess. "Do you know what you want to drink?"

"Water with lime for me," answered Nattie.

"I'll take the darkest beer you have," said Nathan.

"Is Newcastle okay?"

"If that's the darkest you have, then yes."

Nattie smiled playfully. "Can I see if I can guess what you ordered for me?"

"I didn't order what you would have ordered," he announced. He must have noticed her confusion because he immediately amended it to, "I ordered what you would have ordered if price were no object."

Pointing at him she squinted and said, "That, Dr. Watson, may have been too big a hint."

She knew that he would order her seafood, and she noticed that the menu was laid out such that the seafood dishes were all together at the end, but jumping ahead on a menu was not her operating procedure.

He was halfway through with his beer when she got to the bottom of the pasta section. "I'll bet I can guess what you ordered for yourself."

"Take your best shot, Sherlock."

"Creamy turkey and jalapeño pasta," she said.

"How do you do that?"

She looked across the table like she expected him to already know her answer. "Elementary," she finally said.

He slumped back in his chair, knowing he should have seen that coming.

It was just another minute before he knew she had found his selection for her: Chileans sea bass and shrimp scampi.

"It's the most expensive thing on the menu, Nathan."

"I know," he said. "That's why I had to order it."

The waitress came with their orders. Nattie was leaning over hers enjoying the aromas when the waitress asked Nathan if he would like another beer. She was not so much surprised that he ordered a second beer but by how quickly he did.

They ate in relative silence for the next ten minutes. Each moaned appreciatively over the respective meals and did the same when they shared bites across the table. Nattie was no more than a third of the way through hers when the waitress returned to check on them.

"I'm going to need a box," Nattie told the waitress.

The waitress nodded and said, "I hope you saved some room for dessert."

Looking questioningly at Nathan, Nattie said, "I don't know."

"Everyone says we've got to try the giant butterscotch éclair," Nathan told her.

"Can we split it?"

Before Nathan could answer, the waitress said, "Why don't you go check it out? I think there are still a couple left. They're in that dessert cooler by the front counter. You walked by it when you came in."

Nattie retraced her steps across the dining room to survey the dessert display. The butterscotch éclair was the size of a softball and covered in a thick layer of dark chocolate. It was what she would have picked, but there were several other things she would have loved as well. The portions all looked like they were meant to be shared. By the time she returned to the table, there was a box next to her plate and Nathan had a fresh beer next to his.

"So, what do you think?" he asked.

"I think the éclair is the way to go," she answered. "Is that your third beer?"

"I don't know," he said with a tip of his head to the left. "Maybe. Why?"

Because your drinking ruined our marriage and a year ago you were in AA, she thought, but she was not going to spoil the otherwise delightful evening by pushing that old issue.

"I tell you what," he said. "I'm fine, but I'll let you drive back if it will make you feel better."

"What did you decide?" asked the waitress, who suddenly reappeared at their table.

"The éclair," said Nathan, "and two decafe coffees. But let me keep working on my pasta first."

"No problem. I'll go set your éclair aside for you."

172

"I never would have believed it, Nathan, but this place is worth the drive from Bristol. Thank you."

"I'm just glad you like it. I was a little nervous about not trying it myself first, but the people who recommended it were all pretty reliable." Just before popping a fork full of pasta in his mouth he asked, "So, how's work going?"

"Well, I got a certified check from Knox's father yesterday," she told him.

Lifting his beer in a toast he said, "Thank you, Lionel O'Brien." And then he drained the remains of the bottle.

"Yes," she agreed, "he really came through for us."

He waved the waitress over and told her they were ready for dessert. After she cleared their dishes he asked Nattie, "How about your new case?"

"I got a good lead on a good lead," she said.

"I don't believe this," mumbled Nattie with her first bite of éclair still in her mouth.

"What?"

"The filling," she said, pointing at it. "It's homemade butterscotch pudding. It's better than my grandmother used to make."

He chuckled at her as he reached across the table to hold her hand.

She held his hand between her own, studying it intently until they were both quiet again. Then she looked up and asked, "Do you mind a serious question?"

He leaned against the table. "What is it?"

"Do you see me?" she asked. It was a question she was waiting for the right time to ask. Asking it then was more of an impulse than a decision, though.

"What do you mean? Do my eyes look funny or something?"

"No. It's just something I heard Knox say to Kevin the other day. She said she knew her parents loved her, but she doubted they saw her when they looked at her."

"When I look at you, I see the most amazing woman on the surface of the planet. You are the woman I want to talk to, look at, be with. You are the only woman I ever wanted or will ever want. When we aren't together, all I can think about is what is she doing and when will I see her again."

She smiled and said, "That could be a Hallmark card."

"Well, I meant every word," he said before attending to his half of the dessert.

"I know you did," she said, sweetly patting his hand. It might have been the best answer he could muster. There was nothing to gain by telling him that she still did not know if he could see her.

CHAPTER 33

Monday Afternoon: Mary Jane Blackstone

THE GOOD LEAD DID IN FACT LEAD TO A GOOD LEAD. Mary Jane Blackstone was the client Susan was seeing just before her death. She had called Nattie's office that morning and arranged to come Nattie's office that afternoon.

Wet chicken was what Nattie thought when Mary Jane entered her office. Her black hair did not look natural, and it did not complement her pale complexion. Her eyes appeared small, but that might have been because of the darker skin around them. She was tall with a figure somewhere between thin and emaciated. None of her clothes fit. Her jeans were skin-tight, and her calico pullover shirt was so big that the neck hole hung toward her right shoulder.

"Are you the lady detective?" she asked. Her voice had that strained quality that comes from holding your breath while you speak.

"I am. You must be Miss Blackstone," said Nattie as she walked to the doorway and extended her hand.

Mary Jane nodded and looked down at Nattie's hand a moment before putting her own in it. Her hand was cold. She did not squeeze.

"Please come in and sit down," said Nattie. "Can I get you something to drink?"

Mary Jane shook her head no as she sat down across from Nattie's desk. The backpack that she had been carrying in her left hand now rested in her lap. She almost looked like she was trying to hide behind it. "I know who killed Miss Renee," she announced with no discernable change in her expression.

Nattie sat in the chair next to her. "I'd like to hear all about it. If you aren't sure where to begin, then it probably doesn't matter where you begin."

"That sounds like something Miss Renee would say."

Assuming that was a compliment Nattie bowed her head slightly forward.

Mary Jane put her backpack on the floor beside her chair and then drew her knees up to replace it. She wrapped her arms around her legs. In short, she was sitting up in a fetal position. "It was Oddie," she said just barely loud enough for Nattie to hear. "And if he knew I was telling you, he'd be killing me, too."

That was quick and to the point, thought Nattie. "Do you have a last name for Oddie?"

"Pruitt."

"And do you know where Oddie Pruitt is?"

"Oh sure," said Mary Jane, squirming back in her chair. "He's up at Empire."

" 'Empire,' " repeated Nattie. "The maximum-security prison?"

Mary Jane nodded yes.

"What is he doing time for?"

"Do you remember the state trooper who got sniped up on I-81?"

Nattie had not followed that incident very closely, but she remembered reading about it. "That was about a year and a half ago, right?"

"Yeah. Well, that was Oddie."

"And he has been convicted of that, right?"

She nodded yes.

"And what makes you think Oddie killed Susan Renee?"

"I don't think he killed her himself. He was already up at Empire then. I think he got someone else to do it."

"Can you prove that?"

A blank stare crossed Mary Jane's face as she looked back at Nattie without answering.

"That's okay," said Nattie in a soft voice. "Proving it would be my job. What makes you believe he did that? Did he threaten to kill her? Or maybe he had a grudge against her?"

"That's it," said Mary Jane, shaking her thumb toward Nattie.

"He had a grudge," confirmed Nattie.

"Yeah."

"What was the grudge?"

"He hated her."

Nattie stood up and readjusted her chair so that she was sitting squarely facing Mary Jane. When she sat back down, she leaned forward with her elbows on her knees. "Look, Mary Jane, this is the part of your story where I need to get very specific details, so I'm going to ask you questions about what you say, and I don't want you to think that means I think you're lying."

"MJ."

The answer took Nattie back. "I'm sorry."

"Call me 'MJ,'" said Mary Jane. "And I won't be insulted if you don't believe me. Most people don't believe me anyway. I just want to do what's right by Miss Renee. I owe her that much."

"I can see that, MJ," said Nattie.

"So go ahead and ask me your question."

"Why did Oddie Pruitt hate Susan Renee?"

" 'Cause of me. He said talking to her changed me. He thought she made me more mouthy and disrespectful. I think he just didn't like it when I started sticking up for myself."

"And he blamed your counselor for that."

MJ nodded yes.

"Did he ever threaten or confront her?"

"No. He never met her. But he talked bad about her to me."

"Was she afraid?"

"No. I don't think she was afraid at all. The last time he beat me up, she got me into a shelter and she got a restraining paper out against him." Then MJ shook her head slowly back and forth. "But I don't think that paper would have meant much." Looking hard at Nattie she added, "That's why we turned him in about that shooting."

"You turned him in?" clarified Nattie.

"Well, I told Miss Renee, and she did it."

"And that's why you think he might have wanted her killed?"

Her eyes opened wider as she nodded yes.

"I am going to check this out, MJ. It is a very good lead, and I'm going to follow it. But I wonder, how would he know who turned him in?"

She shrugged. "He always had a way of finding out things. I don't know how, but he did."

"I don't mean to alarm you, MJ, but if he was going to blame someone, don't you think you would be the most logical choice?"

"Maybe, but if he thought I did it, he might have blamed her for that, too. Maybe he thinks with her dead and gone, I'll go back to the way I used to be."

"But you won't let that happen, will you, MJ?"

"No," she said without hesitation. "That would be like throwing everything Miss Renee learned me away."

"She really helped you, didn't she?" asked Nattie.

With a stone-cold, unblinking look, MJ answered, "More than anyone ever has."

"This may sound like a strange question, but I wanted to be a counselor for a while, so I'm curious: What did she do that helped you so much?"

MJ continued her expressionless stare into Nattie's eyes as the trace of a smile gently emerged and a distinct warmth animated her eyes for the first time since she arrived. In a soft voice she said, "She believed me."

CHAPTER 34

Doug "Duke" Schneider

"DETECTIVE SCHNEIDER?" ASKED NATTIE ON THE PHONE.

"That is correct," came the response. "And to whom am I speaking?"

"This is Nattie Moreland. You may not remember me, but I'm a PI from Bristol, and we worked on a case together a year and a half ago."

"I remember. That was the Frank Lester case, wasn't it?" he replied. "And didn't you have a kinda funny name like Natasha McSomething?"

"McMorales. Yes, that's me. How are you?"

"I'm getting ready to retire pretty soon. And please, call me 'Duke.' How about yourself?"

"I'm fine, thank you. I was wondering if you could help me with a case I'm working on now."

"If I can, I will. What do you need?"

"I'm working on the case of a social worker named Susan Renee. She was shot in the head out at Steele Creek Park in Bristol. It was deemed a suicide, but we have reason to believe it might have been murder. One of the suspects is doing time up at Empire, but I can't seem to get anywhere with them. Do you have any clout at Empire?"

"It is likely that I have more clout there than you would. What do you need?"

"Our suspect's name is Oddie Pruitt. He's in for shooting that state trooper on I-81. The social worker is the one who tipped off the DA. What I want to find out is if there is any way that Oddie would know who gave him up."

"Actually I think it will be easier to get that info from the DA's office," said Duke. "Can you give me a week? My best connection over there is out of town for a week."

"That'll be fine. Thanks, Duke."

CHAPTER 35

Back at the Office:
A Week Before Rhythm & Roots

"THANKS, JOHN," SAID NATTIE. John Early was the Bristol PD police-man with whom she had the longest positive relationship. Her attempts to get them to reopen the Susan Renee case or at least do a ballistics test had so far been frustrated until she called John Early. She had not called him earlier because she did not want to cash in on their friend-ship unless it came to that. It came to that.

"Is he going to do it?" asked Kevin from just inside her office door.

"He is."

"That's great. I didn't know he had that kind of clout."

"He probably doesn't have enough clout to make someone else do it, but he said he could do it himself and call it practice or skill devel-opment. It wouldn't be official, but it would be enough to force an official test if it's a match."

"Great," he said as he walked across the room to stand in front of her desk. Leaning over he quietly said, "Mrs. Farmer is in the waiting room. She wants to see you. Is that okay with you?"

"Of course. Send her in."

Roberta Farmer entered the room at a trot, scurried across the floor, and collapsed in one of the upholstered chairs facing Nattie's desk. "I know you probably don't want anything to do with us now." She rolled her eyes. "I still can't believe that Mel treated you the way he did."

"He was just doing what he thought was best for his daughter. I understand that. We're all square now."

"Well, that's very generous for you to say."

"Not at all," said Nattie. "What can I do for you?"

Roberta stood up, unfolded a piece of paper she had been holding in her hand, and placed it on the desk in front of Nattie. She said nothing but tapped the paper twice with the tip of her finger.

The note, like the others, was a photocopy of a note made with cutout letters. It read,

THIS IS IT
RHYTHM & ROOTS
I'M COMING FOR YOU

"When did this come?" asked Nattie.

"Yesterday."

Nattie waited for her to settle back in her chair before saying, "I'm not sure why you came to see me, Mrs. Farmer. It seems perfectly clear to me that what you need is a bodyguard."

"I agree," she said, "but we don't know what we're doing. We do want bodyguards for Knox, but we want you to oversee them. We trust you."

Nattie had to smile at that. "I doubt very much that Mr. Farmer trusts me."

"But Knox does. And so do I."

It took a minute but finally Nattie was able to muster, "Thank you."

"Good, then you'll do it."

"I didn't say that yet," Nattie answered with a wave of her hands.

Roberta stood again and handed Nattie a check for $15,000. "I don't know what this will cost, but Knox has a trust fund from her grandfather, and I am the executor. We'll cover whatever you need."

Nattie stared at the check. Looking up she said, "Here's what I'm willing to do. First I'll try to hire a bodyguard. It will be someone I trust to tell me what we are going to need. Then I'll tell you what it's going to cost."

Roberta nodded.

"I'll do that for expenses, which shouldn't be much unless I need to bring someone in. Then, after you hear my proposal, if you want me to proceed I will."

"Agreed," said Roberta eagerly.

"Don't you need to talk to Mr. Farmer first?"

"No. He doesn't need to be involved in this."

"We'll take good care of Knox, Mrs. Farmer," said Kevin from the doorway. His voice had startled Roberta.

The fact that he was standing in the doorway with his arm around Knox startled Nattie.

"Nattie?" It was John Early's voice on the phone.

"John."

"Yeah, well, I got good news for you," he said.

"Are you serious?" said an amazed Nattie. "You got that done this fast?"

"I only had to get a bullet from the gun we had locked up. There was already a ballistics report on the other gun. So all I had to do then was compare them."

"And how did they compare?"

"It's a match. There's no doubt in my mind."

"Oh John," she exclaimed, "thank you. This is great."

"I'm glad I could help. I gotta go, but I'll pass this on upstairs. But, Nattie, you have got to understand something."

"What?"

"The fact that it was the same gun doesn't mean that it wasn't a suicide. She could have killed those DJs and then killed herself later."

"She could have," agreed Nattie. "But she didn't. I can't prove it yet, but it's true."

"Good news," said Nattie when Kevin returned from walking Knox and her mother to their car.

He walked over to the same chair where Roberta had been sitting and slouched in it sideways, throwing his legs up over the right arm. "What's up?"

"We got a break in the Susan Renee case."

"Oh, that reminds me," he said, sitting up. "I've got some new information, too."

"Here's mine," said Nattie. "It was the same gun that killed the WXBQ DJs as killed Susan Renee. Now. What have you got?"

"Okay," he said as he scooted forward in his chair, which meant he was excited about or proud of what he was about to say. "This may not mean much, but a couple of weeks before the WXBQ DJs were murdered she withdrew four thousand dollars from her bank account."

Nattie let that soak in. "What do you think that means?"

"I don't know. But I do know it is unusual. Her finances were as tight as a drum. She might be even more organized than you are."

"What else?"

"Your friend Duke called and said to tell you he's still looking into it, but the tip came from inside that prison. He said you'd know what that meant. Do you?"

"I do. I was wondering if Susan might have been murdered because she tipped off the police about another killing. But I guess that's not it."

"Not so fast," Kevin sang as he shook his finger at her. "I assumed the prison Duke was referring to was Empire, so I got to checking and

I couldn't get much, but I could get at their visitors' log. That's public record."

"And?"

"And Susan Renee visited Empire twice. Once two weeks before she withdrew that money, and then again two days after."

CHAPTER 36

Big Dan Gross

IT WAS ONLY MID MORNING, AND NATTIE was already confused. She sat in her spot at The Grind House trying to assimilate all she had discovered about the Susan Renee case as her chai tea got too cold to drink. On a hunch she had decided to pay a visit to WXBQ that morning to see if she could connect Susan Renee to either Mark Andrews or Steve Stroud. It did not take long. She showed a picture of Susan Renee to the first person she encountered—Debbie, the receptionist—who immediately pointed at the picture and yelled, "That's her. She's the one who was stalking Mark."

Nattie did not recognize him at first. He was a very big man—not quite as large as Beau, but he took up the width of the doorway of the Grind House as he stood surveying the room. When she had last seen Dan Gross, he was one of the most sought-after bodyguards in the Midwest. He was a little thinner back then, but there was no mistaking the silhouette of his head.

"Natasha McMorales," he announced loudly as he crossed the room to where she sat. He knew very well the story behind her name and the ridiculous ethnic hybrid Kevin had saddled her with.

"Shut up," she said as she stood.

He tipped his head back and roared with laughter. He liked to dish it out, and he liked it even more when it was returned. Leaning

187

forward he slid his arms under hers and lifted her off the ground to hug her.

"How are you, Nattie?" he asked, returning her to her feet.

"I'm well, Dan. How about you?"

He held out his left arm. "I suppose you've heard that I retired."

She nodded to affirm that she had heard, as she tried to avoid looking at his arm.

"It's okay to look at it. I think they did a great job on it, don't you?"

She looked more closely at his artificial left arm. Three years ago he was protecting an out-of-control congressman's daughter who flipped her car on Interstate 65 south of Indianapolis. Dan was attempting to pull her from the car when it collapsed on his left arm, severing it just below the elbow. The arm looked real.

Just as she grew self-conscious about staring, he pinched his fingers at her like a crab. He roared again when she jumped.

"Are you okay, Nattie?" asked Samantha from behind the counter.

Dan turned toward Sam. "Is she okay? You want to know if she's okay. It's me who needs protection."

"This man is bothering me," said Nattie.

Pointing at her, "She's bothering me."

"Throw him out," said Nattie.

"Throw her out," repeated Dan.

Samantha rolled her eyes. "Let me know if you want anything."

Dan ordered a large Cowboy Coffee to go.

"I wish you were still in business, Dan. I could use a bodyguard right about now," observed Nattie as Dan sat across the table from her.

"I am working again. That's why I moved here. There's a guy here who's great with prosthetics. He made me this arm."

"Really?"

"Chad McCracken. Do you know him?"

Nattie shook her head no. "How did you find out about him?"

"Actually I came this way to recuperate from the first prosthetic arm I had. An old friend of mine is an occupational therapist here. His name is Brian Miller. We played high school soccer together up in Marion. He and Chad are good friends. I think they're in a Sunday school class together. Anyway, Brian was working with me, and he thought Chad could fix me up so I could actually work again."

"That's great," she said. "Do you have a gun in there?"

He ran his right index finger along his left forearm. "Nine-millimeter. Twelve shots."

Her eyes got big.

He flipped his left hand over and withdrew the plug near the heel of his hand, showing her the end of the gun barrel.

"I thought you were kidding," Nattie confessed.

He frowned. "I wouldn't kid about something like that."

"Of course you would."

"I know," he said with a grin.

"Listen, Dan, I need to be serious. I need you this weekend. I've got a client who's getting pretty threatening notes."

"This coming weekend?"

"Yeah. It's Rhythm & Roots weekend."

"I know, Nattie, but I already have a gig for Rhythm & Roots weekend. April Taylor. She's singing at the Cameo on Friday and Saturday night, but I'm available for Sunday if that helps."

Nattie sighed. "Shoot. Knox is singing at the Grind House on Friday night and Our House on Sunday afternoon. If I can't find anyone for both days, I'll call you."

"Have you tried Emily Garcia out of Kingsport?"

"I ran into Emily over at Cottage Bakery last week. She told me she's now working as an advocate for abused and neglected kids."

"That's interesting," noted Dan with a scratch of his head. "She just started her own line of handmade paracord gun slings. I thought for sure she was still in the business."

Nattie shook her head no.

"How about Courtney Bailey out of Knoxville?"

"I thought she quit and went to law school."

Dan's face scrunched up for a moment, then his eyes got big and he turned toward the counter. "Aren't you Courtney Bailey's big sister?" he asked Robin, who had just delivered coffee to a table in the back.

Robin walked over to them. "Yes."

"Is she still working out of Knoxville, or is she in law school?" asked Dan.

"She did quit to go to law school, but after she had a stalker following her for a while she decided to take on some weekend jobs." Robin smiled, "Mostly she likes taking on stalkers."

"Perfect," said Nattie. "Could you give me her number?"

Robin took out her cell phone, brought up Courtney's name on the contact list, and slid the phone across the table.

"Thanks," said Nattie as she typed the information into her phone.

"I gotta go meet April," Dan said as he stood and picked up his coffee. "We're meeting at the cupcake place across the street," he said, pointing at Shelbee's with his artificial thumb. "I like the coffee here, but the cupcakes there are addictive."

"I know," Nattie agreed. "I have to limit myself to one a week. I usually go on Wednesday afternoons when Stephanie is there doing chair massages."

He stopped grinning and locked eyes with her. "I'm serious, Nattie. If you ever need me, call me."

"I will," she said, placing her hand on his upper arm.

"Careful," he blurted with urgency.

Nattie's eyes enlarged as she withdrew her hand and stared at the spot on his arm where she had touched.

"I shouldn't do that," he said as he tipped his head back and laughed.

CHAPTER 37

Tuesday:
Before Rhythm & Roots

"I DON'T SEE THAT YOU HAVE A CHOICE, NATTIE," pleaded Nathan. "And I don't see what the problem is."

Of course you don't see what the problem is. And you're not going to see what the problem is either. "I know," Nattie said. When it came to Beau Robinette, her thoughts and feelings bounced around like a pinball. He was personable, sensitive, and compassionate, making him easy to engage. He lied to her. More than once. He rescued her when that psychopath Trace Noble attacked her in her kitchen. But he was the one who put her in harm's way in the first place. He was guilty, but she lied to protect him. She lied to send the guiltier Trace Noble away. He would be a great bodyguard. But he made her lie. Rhythm & Roots was just a few days away, and there were no other choices. But she told him if he came back, she would have him arrested. If she asked him to come back now, she would have to lie again. There was nothing else she could do.

"Call him," she said as the muscles on the back of her neck tightened. "He can be here tomorrow night."

CHAPTER 38

Thursday Morning

"Y'ALL GOT ANYTHING TO EAT?" ASKED BEAU as he entered Nattie's office.

"Beau," yelled Kevin. He ran over and hugged the giant man.

"How are you, Kevin?"

"Great. How about you? How's Chattanooga?"

"Chattanooga is a wonderful town. You would love it." Then, looking over the top of Kevin, he eyed Nattie. "But this feels a little like coming home. How are you, Nattie?"

"I'm fine," she said in businesslike detachment. "It is so good of you to help us out."

He eyed her for a moment before saying, "There will never be a time when I would turn down an opportunity to help you."

She did not doubt the sincerity of his statement, but it still made her blanch. She walked over to hug him, more because it would look odd not to than because she felt comfortable doing so. His enthusiasm to hug her was unrestrained as he lifted her off her feet like she was a sack of potatoes.

"Ah, it is good to see you."

"It's good to see you, too." She meant it. "Are you serious about being hungry?"

He patted his stomach. "I don't look this way by accident."

"How much time do we have before Knox gets here?" Nattie asked Kevin.

He looked at his watch, "It's nine now, and she's supposed to be here by nine thirty, so I'd say you have at least an hour."

"But she's worth waiting for, right, Kevin?" chided Beau, draping his left arm across Kevin's shoulders.

Kevin blushed, hardly a common occurrence.

"We've got time to get to Exit 7 and back then, right?" said Beau.

"You do," answered Kevin.

"Great, I heard they built a Chick-fil-A out there since I've been gone."

Kevin pulled back and looked at the big man. "Really? You want Chick-fil-A?"

"Oh yeah," said Beau, "I love their chicken biscuits."

Beau was already in the passenger seat when Nattie slid behind the steering wheel of her Subaru Forester. Her car, which normally felt roomy to her, now seemed crowded.

As they drove onto State Street, she asked, "Why was Kevin so surprised that you'd want Chick-fil-A?"

He looked confused. "I'm gay," he said finally. "I thought you knew."

"No, I didn't," she said.

The awkward silence that followed was broken when she asked, "So, the things the CEO said about homosexuality doesn't keep you from eating their chicken biscuits?"

"Should it?" he asked.

"I don't know," she shrugged. "It sure seemed to upset a lot of people."

"Some people want to get upset. For me, I'm not going to get upset because someone said what he believed."

"But he believes you're wrong."

"I know. But he also believes in treating me fairly. I have friends

193

who work for him and they love him. I'd rather be with someone who thinks I'm wrong but treats me with dignity than with someone who wants to fight for my cause but wouldn't hire me or let me in his house."

39

Friday Night: The Grind House

"HERE," SAID MEL FARMER AS HE HANDED Knox's guitar case to Beau. Their van was parked next to the side door of the Grind House. Knox and her mother were still in the van talking while Mel began unloading her equipment.

"He's not going to carry stuff for you, Mr. Farmer," intervened Nattie.

"Why? There's nothing going on right now. He's on the clock. He should work."

"He needs his hands to be clear," explained Nattie. "We want him to be able to react quickly if it's necessary."

"I'm only talking about a few minutes."

Beau, who had kept his eyes scanning the street while Nattie argued with Mel Farmer, stepped so close to Mel that he had to look almost straight up to see Beau's face. In a very calm but firm voice he told the shorter man, "I'd prefer that you stay out of my way." Then, after holding the eye contact, he said, "Please."

"Sure, no problem," said Mel with the trace of a stutter.

Knox's set went without incident. It lasted fifty minutes and could not have been an easier assignment for a bodyguard. The Grind House stage was at the back of the long room on the other side of the side entrance. Beau could put himself squarely between the audience and the only exit. The maximum audience might have been close to twenty-five, but for Knox it never got above fifteen. Patrons from the coffee shop could hear and enjoy her, and many came down to glance around the corner to get a look at her, but predominantly the audience was small, intimate, and easy for Beau to oversee.

After her show Knox stayed near the stage to speak to some of her fans. Kevin, who had been sitting in the front row, kept his seat and waited patiently, making moony eyes as he watched her.

While Mel packed up the equipment, Roberta stood next to Knox, doing her best to be in the conversation between Knox and whomever she was talking to. While Mel rolled Knox's amplifier by Beau, he overheard Nattie tell him, "Good job," bringing an immediate double take and an expression of disbelief.

40

Courtney Bailey: Saturday Morning

THE SHOPPERS HAVE FREE REIN OF STATE STREET on the Saturday morning of Rhythm & Roots. The vendors are all either open or preparing to open by nine o'clock, and no performances are scheduled for another two hours. The few scattered street musicians are spread out playing solo for donations. They provide a nice backdrop for the shoppers. When the music begins, it becomes shoulder-to-shoulder people on State Street from Piedmont to the State Street stage, so Saturday morning is the time for browsing. The crowd, a fraction of Friday night's crowd, was evenly split between shoppers, vendors, and the festival volunteers, all wearing different colored T-shirts designating their respective area of responsibilities.

Nattie stood in the middle of the street in front of The Grind House surveying the crowd. It was quite a contrast to the craziness of the previous night. She had a 'stop and smell the roses' moment as she watched a team of green-T-shirted volunteers empty garbage containers. It was not that State Street actually smelled particularly fresh, but seeing the City of Bristol come together like this was touching. The festival, in spite of the inconvenience it caused her to have her business blocked off, was good for Bristol. Seeing the volunteers at work symbolized that as much as anything. She took one last scan and silently pronounced her usual morning St. Francis blessing over the town—"Peace and goodwill"—before proceeding into the Grind House to meet with her crew.

"Good morning, Nattie," said Samantha.

"Hi, Sam," answered Nattie. "Did you get any sleep last night?"

"Sleep?" Sam laughed. "What's that? Do you want half-Cowboy, half-decaf?" Samantha took a medium cup and prepared to fill Nattie's order but waited until Nattie nodded her agreement before beginning to pump coffee from their canisters.

"Thanks," Nattie said, taking the coffee and circling to the sugar bar.

Samantha punched in Nattie's name on the cash register. "You have a free one on your account. Do you want to use it?"

As Nattie stirred Splenda into her coffee she looked up and asked, "Why do I have a free one coming? I thought I had two more to go."

Sam threw her thumb over her shoulder, directing Nattie's attention toward the couch where Nathan and Beau were already seated. They each held a mug of coffee and on the table in front of them was a paper Chick-fil-A bag.

They did not notice her approach.

"I don't think I'd trust him that much," said Beau just before Nathan, who was facing forward, spotted her.

Beau strained to turn but broke into a huge smile when he saw that it was her. "Do you want a chicken biscuit?"

"No thanks," she said as she took the chair next to Nathan. "I just had oatmeal. So, Beau, who don't you think you'd trust?"

The two men hesitated and looked at each other.

Eventually Beau conceded the stalemate and shrugged. "I was just asking Nate how the Our House was doing with him taking so much time away and—"

"And," interrupted Nathan, "I told him I was letting Jimmy be the manager."

"And Beau doesn't trust him," repeated Nattie.

"Apparently," said Nathan, looking down.

"Why doesn't Beau trust him?" Nattie asked Nathan.

Nathan scowled at her. "Why are you asking me? He's the one with the trust issue. Ask him."

Nattie knew immediately that she had asked a question that was technically none of her business, but rather than apologize right away—her first impulse—she stared at him. Nathan was not an angry person, so when he lashed out like this, it was usually because he felt cornered or criticized.

Beau broke the silence by standing up. "I'm going to get another coffee."

"Nattie," came a loud voice from the front of the store.

They all turned and watched as a young, dark-haired woman made her way toward them.

"Courtney," exclaimed Nattie as she stood and moved toward the person approaching.

As they hugged, Courtney said, "I'm so glad I found you here. I went over to your office first, but I knew to come here second."

Nathan stood up next to Beau. "We'll leave you two alone."

"Oh, don't go," said Courtney. "This isn't personal."

"Well, let's all sit," said Nattie.

Courtney took the chair across from Nattie and next to Beau.

"Would you like a chicken biscuit?" offered Beau.

"No thanks," answered Courtney. "I'm in town with the Black Lillies. I'm doing their security. They did a show at the Paramount last night, and they have another scheduled for the State Street stage tonight."

"How did it go last night?" asked Nattie.

"The theater was packed and spilling out the door, but security was pretty simple. I had one backstage and one on either side of the staging watching the crowd. The problem is," continued Courtney, "the two

199

guys I had working with me last night are brothers, and they got a call this morning that their parents' paint store in Morristown caught fire sometime last night. They left." She paused before stating the obvious. "I need help."

"Well," said Beau, "you came to the right place." Turning to Nattie he asked, "We're free until tomorrow, right, Nattie?"

"Right," answered Nattie. "What do you need, Courtney?"

"I'd like to have one on either side of the crowd and one backstage."

"I'm in," said Beau.

Courtney smiled and exhaled.

"I can do it, unless you want to," Nattie said to Nathan.

To Courtney Nathan asked, "Can she get the backstage duty?"

Courtney knit her eyebrows together in confusion. "Sure."

"There's a slight possibility that I'm drawing too much attention from the stalker we're investigating," explained Nattie. "But I don't think it's a concern. I'll do whatever you need."

"Well, since it doesn't matter, we'll put you backstage anyway," said Courtney. "So, it's a deal?"

"Deal," repeated Beau and Nattie.

"Great," said Courtney as she stood to leave. "Let's meet back here an hour early. I'll introduce you to the band."

41

Trisha Gene Brady
and the Black Lillies

THE BLACK LILLIES WAS A BAND ON THE RISE. They had just signed with Keith Case and Associates, a big booking agent. They always drew a big crowd in Bristol, and the Friday night performance at the Paramount was packed and lined up out the doors. The band was tight, with Bobby Richards and Jamie Cook holding down the rhythm section as Trisha Jean Brady and Cruz Contreras harmonized.

The Saturday night performance was even more electrifying. The Black Lillies always drew the sunset slot at the end of State Street, so the lighting was just perfect for the elbow-to-elbow audience that was even larger than the Friday night crowd. There were extra musicians on stage sitting in on fiddle and banjo, and the whole atmosphere was like one big party. If anyone in the crowd wasn't singing along with all the songs the band played, Nattie could not find them. At times the crowd was louder than the band.

"Are you okay?" asked Nattie as she approached Trisha Gene Brady. The singer had just come from their second encore. They sang "Little Darling," a crowd favorite. Trisha Gene had belted out her part like it was the first performance of the night. But now she looked like she could barely stand.

"I don't feel so good," said Trisha Gene as she looked around for a place to sit.

"She's fighting off a cold," said Tom Prior. "I told her to take it easy."

Cruz scowled. "There was no way she was going to take it easy. We shouldn't have let her come back out with us."

"How were we supposed to do that? She'd have followed us out."

Nattie, now standing to Trisha Gene's right, held the singer's arm, providing stability more than support. "My office is right over there. I've got a couch, and I can make you a cup of tea or a cup of my grandmother's lemon and honey cure for the common cold. How does that sound?"

Trisha Gene nodded and allowed Nattie to lead her off the stage, across the Rhythm & Roots parking lot, and around the back to the Natasha McMorales Detective Agency office. They made it across the waiting room before Trisha Gene let herself collapse on the couch underneath the print of Botticelli's *Birth of Venus*.

Trisha Gene strained to breathe but did not resist as Nattie felt her forehead.

"You are burning up," noted Nattie.

Trisha Gene forced a weak smile. "I guess that means I'll need your grandmother's concoction."

"Coming right up."

The concoction was a sort of gelatin mixture of lemon and honey. Nattie kept a quart Mason jar of it at home in her fridge and a smaller jelly jar of it in the little refrigerator behind Kevin's desk. A spoonful in a cup of hot water could not be easier to prepare.

They savored the hot elixir in silence. Color came back to Trisha Gene's face, and her breathing was markedly less strained. "That really did the trick," she said as she sat more upright.

"There's something to be said for those old country cures," said Nattie.

"It deserves a song. I'll share this with Cruz."

"That would be wonderful. My granny's not with us anymore, but she'd love that. She'd love your music, too."

"Thank you."

"It seems like you really love what you do," observed Nattie, noting the contrast with Knox, who always seemed indifferent when she performed.

"Oh, I do," said Trisha Gene. "It's my dream job. I started out in college as an art major. I even got an MFA from UT, but five years ago I went with music full-time and I haven't looked back since." She took another long sip from her cup. "So, how about you? Do you like what you do? I never really thought about bodyguards before."

"Well," said Nattie, "I'm not really a bodyguard like Courtney. I'm a private investigator. Courtney and I have worked together several times. In fact, I tried to hire her to help with a stalker case I'm working on here at Rhythm & Roots, but she was already working for you."

"Really," said Trisha Gene. "I guess there are more creeps out there than I thought. I never dreamed I'd need protection until I got a threatening note. It really scared me."

"When was that?" asked Nattie.

Trisha Gene's eyebrows gathered while she thought. "I'm not sure. We spend so much time on the road that it's hard to track time, but it was shortly after those two disc jockeys got killed."

42

Sunday Morning: April Taylor

UNLIKE THE PREVIOUS MORNING WHEN NATTIE crossed State Street from her office to the Grind House, she barely paused to notice the street's activity, much less offer her morning blessing. She was relieved to have the Grind House to herself. She was still digesting the information she had heard the night before from Trisha Gene Brady and all that had happened since.

"That's it," Trisha Gene had exclaimed when Nattie showed her a copy of the note Knox had received. Nattie offered to show her a copy of the second note, but after Trisha Gene hired Courtney Bailey for protection, no more notes came.

Clearly this was a meaningful clue for her investigation. *But what does it mean?* Nattie wondered as she had driven home the previous night. Only her exhaustion had kept her from lying in bed and ruminating on it. *What does it mean?* But she was up at 5:00 a.m. with the question rolling around in her mind.

Five o'clock was early, even for her. But there was no going back to sleep, so she had ambled down to the kitchen to start a pot of coffee. Something stopped her midway down the stairs. It took her a few seconds to realize it was a smell coming from the kitchen.

"Eli," she had yelled out excitedly when she recognized the smell of something baking, which had to mean Eli had finally reappeared.

The potential relief from the anxiety she felt over Eli's unexplained avoidance of her compelled her mad dash down the stairs and to the kitchen, only to find the kitchen empty and the back door open. ·

After scanning all she could see from her back step she returned to the kitchen. With the exception of the clean mixing bowl and utensils drying in the rack by the sink—and the heat and the aroma emanating from the oven—there was no sign that anyone had been there. The timer on the oven was set to go off in twelve minutes, which gave her enough time to go back upstairs and lay out her clothes for the day. When the buzzer sounded she was waiting to remove Eli's handiwork. It was muffins. She bent over them and took a deep breath: piña colada muffins, her favorite. She left them on the counter and went back upstairs to prepare for her day.

It was six thirty when she left her house and began patrolling Eli's stomping grounds. A dozen piña colada muffins stayed warm in a paper bag on the passenger seat of her Subaru. It was seven thirty when the gravitational pull of Trisha Gene's note exceeded her desire to solve the mystery of Eli, and by seven forty-five she was at home in her office, wishing she could talk it all through with Hiram.

At just past eight, Nattie opened the door to the Grind House, still wishing she could talk to Hiram. A full dose of caffeine would be a poor substitute for clarity, but it would go well with the bag full of muffins she held in her right hand.

Samantha and Robin were bent over a game of Uno as Nattie approached the counter.

"Who's winning?" asked Nattie.

"I am," said both women before looking at each other.

"I just won," said Samantha earnestly.

"Yes," agreed Robin with a Cheshire cat grin. "I was winning by three, and now I'm winning by two."

Samantha threw her head back and moaned before looking more closely at Nattie. "Are you okay?"

In response to the question Nattie creased her forehead. "Why do you ask that?" she responded.

Pointing at the top of Nattie's head, "It looks like you're trying to crack a walnut between your eyebrows."

Nattie sat the bag of muffins on the counter and ordered a Cowboy Up coffee. While Samantha got her coffee and Robin rang up her account on the computer, Nattie massaged her forehead with her fingertips. After giving each of them one of Eli's muffins she took her coffee and settled into a table that gave her a good view of her office.

As she peeled away the paper from her muffin, another woman entered the coffee shop. The woman was close to Nattie's age—with a bit more height and the same blond hair, but with a lot more body. Her black dress and several strings of jewelry gave the woman the look of a catalog model. Nattie took a big bite of her muffin as she unconsciously played with her own mousy hair.

An old man with an unkempt beard and a dirty T-shirt followed the catalog model through the door and to her table. When he spoke to her, she jumped slightly but righted herself quickly as she turned to face him. She smiled warmly at him while he spoke. He had her full attention. From where she sat Nattie could not hear what was being said, but when the old man finished, Nattie could read the woman's lips as she responded to him. "Thank you," she told him as she touched his arm.

The old man lit up at her touch and beamed as he scanned the room to see who had noticed. The woman watched the old man head back out on to State Street before scanning the room and then looking at her watch. Whoever she was meeting was still to come.

"You were at the Cameo Friday night, weren't you?" asked Robin.

"That's right," answered the woman.

"We were here," explained Robin, "but I heard it was a great show. I'm sorry I missed it."

An inkling of who the woman was began to form in Nattie's mind.

When the woman sat down, Nattie approached her. "You're April Taylor, right?" asked Nattie as she circled the table.

"I am," April answered, holding out her hand.

The handshake was strong. "I'm Nattie Moreland. I'm a private investigator, and if you don't mind, I'd like to ask you a few questions."

April frowned. "Is something the matter?"

"No, not really. I just happened to know that you hired Emily Garcia for security and—"

April's frown grew more pronounced, and she pulled away in her chair.

"I only know that because I tried to hire Emily for a singer I'm working for," said Nattie, hoping to be reassuring. "So my question is this: Did you hire Emily shortly after the two disc jockeys from WXBQ were murdered?"

April moved back into a comfortable posture in her chair, but her face was still taught. "I did," she said weakly. "Why?"

"Because the woman I work for, Knox DeVilla, got a threatening note just after that happened, and last night I learned that Trisha Gene Brady of the Black Lillies got the same note."

"And you want to know if I got the same note?" asked April.

Nattie nodded yes.

"It was a copy of a note," began April. "There were pictures of Mark Andrews and Steve Stroud at the top, and underneath, it said, 'You're next.'"

They stared at each other. "Is that the same note your client got?" asked April.

"It is," answered Nattie. She already suspected the answer to her next question but asked it anyway. "After you hired Emily, were there any more notes?"

"No, there weren't."

43

Skylar's Reappearance

NATTIE TOOK THE TABLE IN THE ALCOVE to the right of the front door of Manna Bagel while Knox fixed her cup of tea at her usual snail's pace. It was Nattie's normal table, which is probably why Kevin had told her he would meet her and Knox there for lunch.

Nattie had ordered three Natashas for them. A Natasha was an open-faced grilled-cheese sandwich with onion and tomato on a jalapeño bagel. The Natasha sandwich at CityMug was a grilled cheese with tomato and pesto on focaccia bread. Nattie fixed her own coffee and Kevin's, and returned to their table at the front while Knox decided which tea bag to use. *This isn't a race,* Nattie told herself to keep her hurry-up tendency at bay.

"Is that my coffee?" asked Kevin.

Nattie looked up at her brother. She had not seen Kevin enter, but she had expected him. There did not appear to be a reason to answer his question, as he had already picked up the coffee, but all of his attention was elsewhere.

"That's Beau's coffee," she lied.

"Thanks," he said without taking his eyes off Knox.

Nattie reached out and, grabbing his left forearm, directed him down into the chair next to her. "Try not to be so obvious. She's just dunking a tea bag," she advised him.

Once seated he turned to her and said, "But she dunks that tea bag so, so, . . . so."

"Thoroughly," suggested Nattie.

He shook his head slowly. "I'm sorry," he apologized. "I didn't mean to be oblivious."

"You got it bad, don't you, Kevin?"

"What do you mean?" he asked with a frown.

Pointing at his face, she said, "Now you're being oblivious."

His fake frown morphed slowly into an embarrassed grin.

"Before Knox gets over here and I lose you altogether, tell me what you found out from your buddy Dane Kinser. You did get to talk to him, didn't you?"

One of Kevin's favorite songs was a Dane and Taylor song called "State Street." He played it in the office all the time, telling Nattie that since her office was on State Street it should be her theme song. She was fine with that as a theme song, although she had no idea what use she could make of a theme song.

"Oh yeah. I talked to him just a few minutes ago. He was over at the Piedmont stage watching Ed Snodderly and Brandon Story." Kevin did not continue with his report. Seeing he lost Nattie's attention to something behind him, he turned to see that Knox's old boyfriend, Skylar Lynch, had come in and was now sauntering toward her.

Kevin was transfixed as he watched Knox virtually turn around into Skylar's open arms. She did not actually hug him back, but with her arms outstretched she allowed him full access to her. After an excruciatingly long hug, with Skylar's head buried in Knox's hair, he pulled his head back to speak to her. He continued to hold her against himself as he spoke. Knox, for her part, pulled her head back to look at him.

Push him away, Nattie silently pleaded with Knox. Watching her brother, she could see that his mouth was open, but she could not tell if he was breathing.

"I gotta go," Kevin said hurriedly as he stared. After a last look at Knox he headed for the door. "I'll talk to you later."

After exiting he paused on the sidewalk to look both ways. His only thought had been to leave, so now he had to think about where to go. He chose to the right toward their office. He did not look inside as he passed by the window.

Nattie had followed his movements with her eyes until he passed by out of sight. When she turned back to face the room, she was surprised to find that Knox had followed Skylar to a table across from the cash register.

Nattie fumed. Anger was not a familiar emotion for her, but hurting her little brother was the surest way to get her riled. That is the way it would be for any momma bear. What to do with her anger did not dawn on her until she watched Carol come from behind the counter to bring the three Natashas she had ordered. She opened her bag and searched through a smaller compartment inside. She found what she was looking for and held it hidden in her palm until Carol had deposited the three sandwiches and left.

Once she was alone, Nattie emptied the contents of a saltshaker onto a napkin. Then she fit the object in her hand inside the glass and refilled it with salt. A quick examination of her handiwork with the saltshaker satisfied her, so she stood up and, taking two of the sandwiches, she headed over to Knox's table.

"I brought your lunch," Nattie said as she placed one of the sandwiches on their table.

"Thank you," said Knox weakly. She glanced up at Nattie but did not hold eye contact for long.

You should be embarrassed, scolded Nattie silently.

Skylar did not look at Nattie at all. He did help himself to half of Knox's sandwich.

"Do you mind if I borrow your salt?" asked Nattie. "There isn't any at my table."

Skylar picked up the saltshaker and held it up, still without looking at Nattie.

With no one watching, Nattie needed no stealth to switch the two salts. She sat the one with her device inside on the table between them and excused herself. Once she was back at her table, she fitted the receiver earpiece into her ear and turned on the receiver.

"Why would I trust you again?" asked Knox.

"Why would anybody trust anybody?" retorted Skylar.

Pause.

"Look, baby, I know I hurt you, but that girl didn't mean anything to me."

"That doesn't make it better."

Good for you, cheered Nattie to herself.

Pause.

"That's not fair," he continued. "We weren't together then."

"We were together the day before."

"We were together the day before, but we weren't back together. If we were back together I'd never have cheated on you."

"Why?"

"What do you mean 'why'? I just wouldn't."

"Why do you want to be with me anyway?"

Pause.

Knox continued, "When you look at me, Sky, what do you see?"

"What do I see?" he repeated.

"Yes, Sky. When you think of me, what do you think? Who am I to you?"

"That's easy," he said in a lower, more breathy voice. "When I think about you I picture you in that white bikini. The one you wore when we went to Myrtle Beach that one time. I think about your hair and the way the wind would catch it when we were playing in the waves."

"In the white bikini," interjected Knox.

"Yeah," he answered excitedly. "I love the way other guys look at us when we're together."

You're not buying this, are you? wondered Nattie as she listened.

"So you like the way I look," noted Knox. "Anything else?"

"Anything else?" he repeated.

Pause.

"I love the way you feel in my arms."

Are you guessing? questioned Nattie as she noticed his voice get higher at the end of the sentence.

"And I love the way your bottom lip pouts out when I kiss you."

Pause.

"So," he said, "what do you think?"

Pause.

"I think you're an idiot," she answered without hesitation.

"What?" he asked, sounding like he had a golf ball in his throat.

"There was a time when I thought I could not live without you, but sitting here right now, I don't know why I ever thought that."

"Are you serious?"

"Very serious. And now I know. I need more than that. I want more than that."

"Is there someone else?" he asked. He sounded angry.

"As a matter of fact there is someone else, but that has nothing to do with this. You were my first love, and I'll always love you for that. And until just now I wasn't entirely sure that I was over you."

"And now you are?"

"Now I am," she said. "I'm sorry if that hurts you, but I need more."

"And this guy, how is it he gives you more than I do?"

"Because," she said as she pushed away from the table and stood up, "when he looks at me . . . what he sees is me!"

44

Sunday Afternoon Powwow

"I DON'T WANT TO TALK ABOUT IT," ANNOUNCED KEVIN as he entered Nattie's office.

"Just sit down, Kevin," Nattie instructed. She stayed seated behind her desk as she held out a small white paper bag.

"What's that?" he asked.

"It's your sandwich."

"I don't want it," he huffed as he collapsed into one of the chairs facing her desk.

"Yeah, Kevin, don't eat. That'll show her."

He did a double take. That she could be sarcastic was no news. She was world-class in the sarcasm department, but the timing was completely unexpected. He stared blankly at her.

"I know what you saw was upsetting, but in the end she told him she was with someone else."

He leaned forward against his knees and strained his eyes. "How do you know? Did she tell you that?"

"Just trust me, Kevin. I know what I'm telling you. Do you think I'd tell you something like this if I wasn't sure? That would be like rubbing salt in your wound." She grinned at her double entendre and immediately wiped the smile off her face lest he get too curious.

"I know what I saw, Nattie. That guy was all over her."

"He was."

"And she didn't do anything about it."

"She didn't do anything about it right away."

Kevin huffed again and slumped back in his chair.

"Look, Kevin, it was not cool to let that guy do that, but it doesn't mean what you think it means either."

"Really," he said, but he did not want an answer.

"Yeah, really. You've met her parents. Do you think she was raised in a way that would allow her to have boundaries, much less protect them?"

He sat up and gave her his full attention.

"Believe me, Kevin. She pushed him away."

"Did she tell you that?" he asked, this time wanting an answer.

"No, she didn't. And don't ask me how," she warned him with a finger and a stern look, "but I heard her do it."

"Is that legal?" Kevin asked.

"Is what legal?" asked Nathan from the doorway.

"Nothing," answered Kevin quickly without breaking eye contact with Nattie.

Before Nathan settled into the other chair across from Nattie's desk, Nattie directed Kevin back to the Manna Bagel bag with her chin. As Nathan sat, Kevin rose and retrieved the bag.

"Do you want half a Natasha?" Kevin asked Nathan.

"Sure," Nathan answered. As he reached in the bag he asked, "Is this a CityMug Natasha or a Manna Bagel Natasha?"

"Manna," answered Nattie, but the attention of the men across from her was elsewhere. "I'm going to get Hiram on the phone while you guys finish that."

Both men nodded their approval while chewing. A childhood memory crossed Nattie's mind. She was seven and her grandfather, the Wolf, had taken her to the monkey house at Brookfield Zoo. The memory she revisited was of two monkeys sitting next to each other munching on bananas. *We've come a long way,* she mused.

"Is everybody there?" asked Hiram. Nattie had seen that the call was from him and put him on speakerphone right away.

"Beau's catching a show at the Mural, but Nathan and Kevin are both here," answered Nattie.

"Okay," said Hiram. "What's new?"

Nattie pointed at Kevin, who swallowed hurriedly and waved her off because of it.

"Kevin has some information from his friend. Isn't that right, Kevin?"

Kevin wiped his mouth. "Yeah, I talked to Dane Kinser this morning."

"And what did you find out?" prompted Hiram after a few seconds of silence.

"Oh, right," laughed Kevin, bumping his forehead with the palm of his hand.

"Dane says his wife, Lauren, got one of those notes, too, but she didn't get another one either. She's a singer, too."

"And what did they do?" asked Nattie.

Kevin grinned. "Dane just laughed when I asked him that. He said, 'If you knew my wife, you'd know all she did was laugh and say, "I'm next? Sure I am,"' as she wadded it up."

"Slow down a minute," demanded Hiram. "Which note are we talking about?"

"That first note that Knox got. The one with the pictures of the DJs. It said, 'You're next,'" answered Nattie.

"And she did get one," confirmed Hiram. "But she just threw it away and never got another note."

"Right," said Kevin.

"'Either,'" Hiram said. "You said, 'She didn't get another note either.' What does that mean?"

"I can answer that," stated Nattie. "Last night I was with Trisha Gene Brady, the female singer with the Black Lillies, and found out that she got that same note. And then earlier today we ran into another female singer, April Taylor. She got the same note."

"Did she get another?" asked Hiram.

"No," said Nattie. "That's why I told Kevin to talk to his friend. I knew he was married to a female singer."

"So what do we know?" asked Hiram.

Nattie held up one finger. "We know at least four female singers got the same note."

"More than that," said Nathan. "Annie Robinette played at Our House last night. She was with two other women: Kim Lyons and Beth Snapp. They called themselves Girls with Guitars."

"Did they all get notes?" asked Hiram.

"No, only Annie. She said she just thought April Taylor sent the note, so she threw it away because she said, and I quote, 'April knows I sit in the rocker on my porch with a shotgun in my lap.'"

Hiram gave them no time to enjoy picturing Annie Robinette sitting on her porch. "Do we know if any men got the note?"

"Brandon didn't, and neither did Dane nor Taylor," answered Kevin.

"And neither did any of the men from the Black Lillies," added Nattie.

"But," blurted Kevin, "not every woman at Rhythm & Roots got one either."

"Do you know something else?" asked Nattie.

"Yeah, as I was coming back here I walked by Sessions 27, and the three women from Red Molly were in there taking pictures with the owners, Con and Nancy Sauls. So I went in and asked if any of them got notes. They didn't."

"'Red Molly,'" repeated Hiram. "Are they local?"

"No," answered Kevin. "New York."

"I don't like this," said Hiram. "I don't like this at all."

"What is it, Uncle Hi?" asked Nathan.

"I knew it," scolded Hiram through the speaker. "I knew it was a bad sign when Nattie got that threat on her phone instead of the singer's phone." After moaning he added, "I wish I had listened to myself back then."

"What are you saying?" asked Nathan.

"I'm saying it's Nattie," answered Hiram.

The three in Nattie's office stared blankly at each other until Nathan's posture got stiffer and his eyes got bigger. He stood up and pointed at Nattie. "He's saying it's you, Nattie. You're the target."

45

Digging In

NATHAN, WHO WAS STILL STANDING and pointing at Nattie, slowly lowered his hand. "We all should have listened to you back then, Uncle Hi."

"Look, gentlemen," Nattie barked in an attempt to reestablish her authority. "I appreciate your concern, but right now we need to stay focused on protecting our client, which is Knox. Not me."

Nathan sat down, which she expected. Hiram, however, persisted, which she also should have expected.

"Let's examine that, shall we?" said Hiram. "First, Knox gets a threatening note, but at least five others get the note, too. Right?"

"Right," answered Nathan quickly.

"Second," continued Hiram, "all the notes are sent to singers, but only female singers, right?"

"Yes, but what does that mean?" asked Kevin.

"For now, let's just lay out what we know, and then we can ask what it all means," answered Hiram. "Third, only local female singers got notes."

"Black Lillies are out of Knoxville," observed Nattie.

"That's still fairly local," said Kevin, "and Red Molly is out of New York and none of them got notes."

"Now," said Hiram, "what makes local female singers different from male singers or out-of-town female singers?"

Nattie, Nathan, and Kevin looked back and forth between the three of them.

Hearing no response Hiram answered the question himself. "Local female singers are more likely to hire a local female detective."

"That's a stretch, isn't it?" reacted Nattie.

"Is it?" responded Hiram. "Let's push it further, shall we? Of the five local female singers who got the first note, which one got a second note?"

Nathan pointed at Nattie and stood up again.

Before he could speak, Nattie cut him off with a shake of her hand. "I know what you're going to say. The only one who got a second note is the one who hired me."

"You have to admit that's pretty significant," Kevin pleaded.

"Significant, yes," she admitted. "But is it enough to say for sure that I'm the target and that Knox is under no threat?"

"I'll answer that," said Hiram. "It's not enough to say Knox is out of danger, but it is enough to say that you are in danger."

Nattie looked at the two men sitting across from her. Each looked somberly back at her.

"Okay," she acquiesced. "What do you propose we do?"

"Nattie, until we know more, you dig in at your office. Nathan, you go get Beau. I know you want to stay with Nattie, but Beau is better equipped to handle this."

"No problem. I understand. I just want what's best for her," said Nathan.

"What about me?" asked Kevin.

"Let Nathan trade places with Beau, but when Beau gets to the office you should join Nathan on the Knox detail."

Kevin nodded, which Hiram could not see, and stood up announcing, "I'm hitting the head."

"Are all agreed?" asked Hiram.

"Ten-four," answered Nathan.

Under her breath so that Hiram could not hear, she asked Nathan, "Are you okay handling Knox without Beau?"

Nathan nodded yes.

"Nattie, are you in agreement with this plan?" asked Hiram.

"I am," she answered.

"Good. I have to go to physical therapy now but I'll have my phone, so call me if anything changes."

So if someone breaks into my office to attack me, I should call you so that you could begin getting a medical discharge going, thought Nattie. "Don't worry, we'll keep you posted."

"Dig in," repeated Hiram as he hung up.

"You're like his daughter, you know," said Nathan as she walked him out. At the door he stopped and hugged her. "Lock the door behind me."

She nodded yes against his chest.

"And don't let anyone in without checking who it is."

"I know, Nathan."

"Are you armed right now?"

Letting go of him she took a half step back and looked up. "I'll be okay. Really. I know what to do. Besides," she added, putting her hand softly against the middle of his chest, "we aren't perfectly sure that the target is me."

It's me. Is it me? It could be me. The thoughts kept circling around in her mind. They were thoughts she needed to reckon with, but she was not prepared to think clearly about them, at least not yet. *Is it me?* she thought again in spite of herself. *I can't deal with this now. When Beau gets here, I'll be ready.* Standing over Kevin's desk she found herself staring at the blinking light on the phone. It took a moment for it to sink in that the flashing light meant there was a message. Thankful for the diversion Nattie pushed the button.

"Hi, Nattie. Duke Schneider here," began the recording. "I have that information you wanted about your social worker. I know who she visited up at Empire twice, and I can confirm that he is also the one who made the deal for early release. Your guess is as good as mine about his involvement in any of those murders, but Nattie, I want you to be careful. You know this guy. You helped send him away. It's Trace Noble."

46

Eli

NATTIE HEARD THE MESSAGE WITH PERFECT CLARITY, but she needed to play it again just to be sure she heard it correctly. As she held out to push the replay button, the shake in her hand drew her attention. Not wanting to notice the tremor she quickly pushed the button and shoved her hand into her pocket.

The message was the same. Trace Noble was out of prison. He was probably the one who killed the two DJs, and if so, then he probably killed the social worker, too. He probably sent all those threats to local female singers. And if he did that, then Nattie was surely the target.

She took out her Ruger and placed it on the desk next to the phone while Duke's message finished playing. Next she took out her phone and called Beau. Ten minutes ago she would have told him to stay put until after Knox's show, but now she wanted him to come ASAP.

"It's me, Nattie," she said into Beau's voicemail. "Call me as soon as you can. I know who we're dealing with now. It's Trace Noble."

After hanging up she stood frozen wondering what to do next. *Breathe,* she told herself. She took three slow, deep breaths before picking up her Ruger. Placing her trigger finger alongside the barrel, she slid it back, chambering a cartridge. Her next exhale was deliberately loud. She wanted to hear herself breathe. Keeping her finger away from the trigger she walked over to the door to recheck the lock. She knew Nathan had locked it when he left, but she needed something to do.

The door was locked. She could see that it was locked, but she reached for it anyway. *Get a grip,* she told herself as she grasped the handle. The pun brought a slight smile to her face. She was still grinning when the doorknob turned beneath her grip.

Nattie's left hand reflexively opened and hovered an inch above the doorknob. Her right hand came up as her finger slid over the trigger. Cupping her left hand under her right, she cradled her gun while taking one step back and to her right. The first thing whoever came through that door was going to see would be the business end of her weapon.

Everything slowed, though nothing moved. Then the door opened about a foot and was immediately followed by a man's foot. The foot wedged against the bottom of the door while two hands pulled back at the key, which was stuck in the lock.

A man's voice said, "I hate it when inanimate objects refuse to cooperate." It was Kevin's voice. When he finally freed the key and took one step into the waiting room he found Nattie still standing in a shooter's posture and holding the gun with both hands.

"Shit!" yelled Kevin as he threw himself backward.

Eli had been standing behind Kevin and caught him as he fell backward. At that point Eli had not seen Nattie, so he had no idea of why Kevin fell. He just stood there looking down at him with each of his hands under Kevin's armpits. Kevin's torso was suspended about eighteen inches off the ground until Eli looked up and saw Nattie himself. "Shit!" he exclaimed as he stood up and held his hands out in surrender.

"Shee-it," drawled Kevin after he hit the floor. "Nattie, what are you doing?"

Nattie stepped over Kevin. Grabbing Eli by the middle of his shirt she pulled him past her into the room. While she did all this she kept one eye and the gun focused on the open door. She then scanned the parking lot. Seeing nothing she closed and dead bolted the door.

"Let's sit down," she said as she turned around.

As she said this, Eli was standing over Kevin. Their hands were locked, and in another second Kevin would have been pulled to his feet. The request to "sit," however, caused both men to freeze and do a double take.

"Oh, get up," she said as she holstered her gun. Pointing at the couch she said, "Sit over there. Something has happened, and I have to call Beau."

While Nattie retried calling Beau, Kevin and Eli took their assigned places on the couch.

Nattie huffed as she hung up the phone. Beau was still not answering his phone. She sat on the edge of the couch so that she could see both Kevin and Eli. Eli sat in the middle.

"So, what happened?" asked Kevin.

"I know who we're dealing with now," said Nattie. "It's Trace Noble. He got out of Empire in the spring."

Kevin's face softened and his eyes, which had been locked into Nattie's, shifted to Eli. Kevin put his left hand on the back of the younger man, who had slumped forward to the point that his face was completely out of sight.

"What's going on, guys?" asked Nattie, her voice in a higher pitch.

"It's all my fault," mumbled Eli.

"It's not your fault," said Kevin, rubbing Eli's back.

"If you two know something I need to know, I'd appreciate someone letting me in on it."

Eli lifted his head. His eyes were red. "Is the guy you just mentioned the same one from your kitchen?"

Nattie nodded yes.

"Does he have aces tattooed on his fingers?"

"That's Trace," she said. "Why?"

Eli swallowed hard. "He came to see me up at Livingston."

Nattie's face grew tight. Her eyebrows furrowed. "When?" she asked through a clenched jaw.

Eli squirmed. "I don't know. It was a while ago."

"Do you remember when you came to see me in the spring?" she asked. "Nathan thought you were hurting me."

He sat up a little taller and pointed at her. "It was right after that."

"What did he want, Eli?"

"He wanted to know who hit him. He knew it wasn't you, and he didn't believe it was me." A single tear slowly rolled down Eli's left cheek. "I didn't want to tell him. He said he was going to kill me and then he was going to kill my mother."

Beau Robinette's picture popped into her head. The big man had both saved and complicated her life that day. The urgency to raise him on the phone just doubled, but for Nattie, attending to Eli was the first order of business. She placed her right hand on top of his left hand, which was trembling with a fistful of his baggy pants. "Is that why you have been avoiding me, Eli?"

Eli did not answer, but he looked Nattie square in the eyes for the first time.

"Look," Nattie continued, "you did what you had to do to take care of yourself and your mother. I don't blame you, and neither will Beau."

Kevin broke the silence. "I'm just curious," he asked. "How come he didn't believe it was you who hit him? That's what the paper said happened."

Eli slumped back into the couch and hid his face behind his left arm. His speech was choppy, and it sounded like he was holding his breath or fighting off tears. "He told me I was too weak. Then he made me beg and I started crying." The tears began to flow. "Then he pointed his gun at me and pulled the trigger. It wasn't loaded, but I was so scared, I peed all over myself. He just laughed at me and said, 'You see how weak you are.' He said he knew I was too weak to have knocked him out with a baseball bat."

"Hey, man," said Kevin while placing his hand on Eli's shoulder. "Maybe baseball isn't your game."

Eli stopped crying. Both he and Nattie looked at Kevin in disbelief.

Kevin shrugged. "What? Maybe golf's his game."

47

Digging Out

EVERYTHING BECAME CLEAR TO HER as soon as she hung up her phone. It was not just what had been happening and why, but also what she needed to do next. It all clicked into place for her when Nathan called to tell her that Beau was missing.

"What is it?" asked Kevin. He was seriously studying Nattie's face.

"That was Nathan. He needs you down at Our House. Beau is on his way here, and Knox's show is going to start in half an hour."

"What about you?" he asked.

"I'm fine, really. I'm dug in here, and Beau is on the way. Take Eli with you, and when her show is over, everybody will meet back here for another powwow."

"Let's go," Kevin said to Eli, tapping the tall kid on the chest with the back of his hand.

Eli looked at Nattie. It was a look she interpreted as asking for permission, so she nodded and said, "It's okay, Eli. Go on with Kevin."

As soon as Kevin and Eli turned the corner onto State Street and disappeared into the crowd waiting for the Sam Bush concert to begin, Nattie trotted out and around the building. Because of Rhythm & Roots she had parked her car in the YMCA parking lot. As she trotted up the hill she heard Sam Bush tell his fans, "I spend half my life tuning my mandolin and the other half playing it out of tune."

The drive home did not take much longer than her trip up the hill. She drove by the front of her house and noted the unfamiliar white van parked on the street. Driving around the block she parked and approached the rear of her home through her neighbor's yard.

The first thing Nattie noticed when she opened the back door and stepped into the kitchen was how dark it was. It was late afternoon and all the lights were off, but still, she had plenty of windows. There was also an ominous heaviness in the air, but she expected that.

Slow and thorough, she reminded herself as she scanned the kitchen to make sure it was clear. The dining room was next. If Trace were to hide in the dining room, his options were behind the door, under the table, or on the other side of her grandmother's hutch. She cleared all of these spots from the doorway. As she stepped fully into the dining room she could see into the middle of the front room. That is when Beau came into view.

From the dining room Nattie had a side view of Beau. He was tied to the chair adjacent to her sofa. His arms were along the side of his body. The rope that tied him was wound around and around his torso, pinning him against the back of the chair. His head was slumped forward. He was not moving.

Moving slowly across the dining room Nattie kept scanning back and forth. Trace was somewhere. Until she knew where he was, she could not let her guard down for anything.

At the edge of the front room she stopped to listen. The dim light that shone through the maroon curtains upped the eeriness factor that was already well beyond her tolerance. All she could hear was Beau's labored breathing. *Breathe,* she reminded herself as she listened.

She flinched when Beau's head twitched, fell backward, and bounced back into the slump. That is when she noticed his mouth was taped shut, his left eye was swollen shut, and there was dried blood under his nose.

As much as she knew to keep her head, she could not stop the flood of images that crashed through her mind. The images made her angry: Trace beating a tied-up Beau, humiliating the teenaged Eli, the groping of Beau's niece, and the deaths of the two WXBQ DJs and Stacey Renee's sister. When the thoughts turned to the memory of him attacking her in her own home, the feeling also turned. The memory of him touching her, whispering in her ear, and nibbling on her neck as he trapped her against himself brought a feeling of disgust. She felt like vomiting.

All of those thoughts disappeared the instant Beau's head began to twitch again. This time he seemed more awake. More in pain. More afraid. He turned his head to the left only slightly, but immediately his whole body convulsed in pain.

Nattie ran across the room and stood next to him. Holding her gun with one hand she tugged at the ropes with the other, but when his head and shoulders slumped forward she had to shift around in front of him as her left arm was not strong enough. She placed her gun on the coffee table behind her and lifted his head gently with both her hands.

Before she could decide what to do next she sensed his presence. He was rushing at her from behind. There was just enough time to turn her body back toward the coffee table where her gun was, but not enough time to reach it. He tackled her, driving his head and shoulder into her midsection. Outweighing her by a good eighty pounds gave him more than enough power to not only take her off her feet but to propel her through the air and onto the sofa.

She actually heard the air being knocked from her as he landed on top of her. It took several attempts at breathing to finally get enough oxygen in to begin thinking clearly again. She swung her right elbow backward at his face, but his right arm was in the way. After wiggling herself underneath him she reached up with both hands attempting to dig at his eyes, but he was too strong. He swatted her hands away and pressed his left hand down on top of her chest. She struggled to breathe as she helplessly watched the white rag in his right hand cover her nose and mouth. The smell curled her lips and she tried not to breathe, but that was not going to work for long. And it did not.

48

Why Nattie?

IT WAS LIKE COMING OUT OF A TRANCE. She must have been aware that he was slapping her and calling her name for a while, because when she finally responded she was aware that it had been going on for some time. For the first few moments of consciousness she was only aware of being slapped. Who was slapping her was the next awareness to come into focus. This was quickly followed by fear—then a struggle, which brought the awareness that she was tied up with tape across her mouth—and terror finally settled in.

Trace Noble sat on the edge of the coffee table. He was facing Nattie. When she began to struggle he leaned back to watch, and when she finally froze in terror he roared with laughter.

"I'm going to give you a few minutes to wake up, sugar," Trace sneered at her. "I want your full attention when we talk." Turning to Beau he added, "Ain't that right, big fella?"

Beau looked back at him. His left eye was completely swollen shut, and his right eye was only slightly better, twitching under the strain of trying to stay open.

Trace laughed again and then, leaning closer to Nattie, he said, "I guess he can't talk right now."

Instinctively Nattie leaned back and away from him. The movement brought instant pain. Her arms were tied behind her such that leaning back torqued her elbows and shoulders. She looked down at the binding around her middle, and for the first time she noticed that her blouse had been torn open. This brought another wave of fear and another wide-eyed stare into Trace Noble's face. She was at his mercy and had hoped to see mercy in his eyes.

Trace was enjoying himself.

"Here's what's going to happen, sugar," began Trace. "I'm going to take that tape off your pretty mouth, and we're going to have a conversation." Reaching to his left on the coffee table he picked up a large, very shiny knife. He ran the side of the blade gently across her cheek. She could feel the coldness of the steel. Then he said, "And you are not going to scream out, are you?"

Unable to answer, Nattie watched in horror while he lifted the knife over her head and jammed it down into her thigh. It was just a puncture wound, so the act scared her more than hurt her.

"Good," he said. "I see I got your attention. Now I'm telling you, if you don't stay quiet, then I'm going to drive this down to bone." He led the knife blade in front of her so that she could see her own blood on its tip.

"So, I want you to understand something first." His smile was sickeningly smug as he wiped the blood from the knife on Nattie's jeans. "You are dead. And the big guy here, he's dead, too. By the time anyone finds your bodies, I'll be in Charlotte, and by tomorrow morning I'll be in the Cayman Islands." With that he tore off the tape from Nattie's face.

Nattie flexed her jaw as she watched him lift the knife above her leg.

"Quiet now," he warned her again.

"What do you want?"

"A decision, sugar. I want you to make a decision."

Nattie stared at him.

"You're the one who brought the heat down on me, but I'd have still gotten out of here if it weren't for him. So I figure I have to treat you differently." He leaned close again, "You see, I'm going to torture one of you, but not both of you. And you, sugar, get to decide."

"Torture me, you pig."

This brought another wave of laughter. "Gladly, but you need to hear the rest of it. If I torture you—and believe me, sugar, that's what I want you to pick—it will be painful. But if I do torture you, I'll make him watch before I kill him."

"You're a sick pig," she said.

"Maybe so, but I'm the sick pig with the knife, so let's have your decision."

"How do I know that you aren't going to torture me first and then, when I'm dead, torture him anyway?"

"I'd say you're just going to have to trust me, sugar." He leaned back and grinned.

Nattie heard a noise, somewhere between a pop and a thump, and the grin disappeared from Trace's face. His eyes bulged out, and his body surged forward for an instant before convulsing and throwing him backward over the coffee table.

Nattie looked directly over Trace's motionless body at Eli, who stood breathing heavily as he stared down. In Eli's hands was the driver from Nattie's golf bag in the kitchen.

With a deep sigh, Eli looked down at the club in his hands and said, "I guess Kevin was right. Maybe golf is my game."

Epilogue

NATTIE STOOD IN FRONT OF THE GRIND HOUSE, the day's mail in her hand, peering in at what was once her table. She hated that it was closed. Diagonally across from her office it could not have been more convenient. The coffee was great, and the staff all knew her. It was homey for her.

Everything changes, she sighed to herself as she turned to begin the two-block walk up State Street to CityMug. Downtown Bristol had changed for the good over the last decade, but more recently several stores had closed. Sessions 27 was now a dress shop, Pretty Girl Station. Ryland Jewelers was closed, and the Fabric Gallery was closing.

Her phone rang as she crossed Moore Street.

"Hey, girlfriend," came the enthusiastic voice of Beau Robinette.

"Beau," she said, louder than she meant, drawing some startled looks from two power-walking women who were passing her.

Nattie and Beau had not spoken in the last month. For the first two weeks after their ordeal in her living room, they were together nearly every day while they convalesced. Instead of going back home to Chattanooga after that, Beau had headed to New Orleans, where he lived before Katrina hit.

"I'm fine," he answered, emphasizing the word "I'm." "I'm home now. I didn't really need all that time off, but it sure felt good. How about you? Back at it, I assume?"

"You're fine," repeated Nattie. "Who's not fine, Beau?"

Beau sighed. "I was trying to work up to that, but since you are already there, it's Nathan."

It had been two days since she had heard from Nathan, which she had noted because it was so unusual, but she had not been alarmed until Beau asked the question.

"I'm heading downtown to meet him for lunch right now. Is there something I should know?"

"I don't know for sure," answered Beau. "I got a call last night from Our House. He hadn't been in all day."

"He was probably just upstairs in his apartment. Did anyone from the bar go up and check?"

"Several times, and they even went in his apartment around eight o'clock. He wasn't there. That's when they called me. I've been calling him since then, but he's not answering." An awkward silence passed before Beau continued, "But you're going to meet him now, right?"

"I am," she answered weakly as she arrived at the CityMug door. She turned to face herself in the window. *What are you doing?* she thought to herself as she stood with her phone against her ear. An all-too-familiar, sick-to-her-stomach feeling began to gnaw at her. She swallowed hard. "Listen, Beau, I'm about to go inside. I'll talk to you later, okay?"

"No problem," he said. "Keep me posted."

She slid her phone back into her shoulder bag and looked past her reflection, hoping to see Nathan waiting for her.

Kevin and Knox were sitting on the couch, facing the window Nattie looked through. Assuming she was watching them, they began to perform for her. Kevin made the fish face he thought of as his signature pantomime. Knox, of course, thought it was genius and countered with her own rendition of a monkey. Neither noticed Nattie not noticing.

They were cuddling when Nattie steeled herself enough to walk in and take the upholstered chair next to the couch. "This must be the land of romance," she said halfheartedly.

"And all is well," heralded Kevin.

Knox tightened her eyebrows as she looked at Nattie. "Are you okay?" she asked.

Tempted to say, "Sure," Nattie caught herself. There was a simple straightforwardness in the way Knox looked at her. "I'm a little worried about Nathan," she revealed. "I haven't heard from him in a couple of days, and Beau just called to say he was AWOL yesterday."

Kevin looked at his watch. It was eleven forty-five. "He's meeting us for lunch, right? He's only fifteen minutes late. That's normal for him, isn't it?"

True, thought Nattie. She had always been the punctual one in their relationship.

"He'll be here any minute," said Kevin confidently. "We'll wait."

Knox, who was sitting on the other side of Kevin from Nattie, flinched and looked at him suspiciously when he pronounced that Nathan was only late.

Nattie looked at her watch. "I'd say we could give him fifteen more minutes, but if he doesn't make it by noon, I say we go on without him."

Maggie Lawson, whom Nattie had met doing security for a Miss Virginia pageant, came in wearing a CityMac T-shirt. Nattie went over to say hello. She was only gone for a moment as Maggie was late for work, but when she returned Kevin and Knox were once again lost in the land of romance.

Nattie was relieved that she did not have to make small talk. She opened the first of her letters. It was a thank-you card from Stacy Renee and included a final check. She placed the folded check into her bag without looking at it and began reading the note. The note brought a temporary smile to Nattie's face.

The next three letters were advertisements she did not open. The last letter surprised her. It was from Knox's grandmother. Instead of sending her a bill, Nattie had written a letter to inform her that since Nattie and not Knox had been the target, there would be no more payments expected.

"I got a nice letter from your grandmother," announced Nattie.

"Really," responded Knox, looking a bit surprised.

"Did you open that?" asked Kevin, looking at the unopened letter.

Nattie opened the letter as they watched. Inside was a bill on the Natasha McMorales Detective Agency letterhead, and attached to the bill was a cashier's check for $3,500.

Nattie held up the check. "What's this?"

"Don't be mad," pleaded Knox. "I know what you told her, but I told her to pay it anyway. It's not your fault he picked me to target. We thought I needed protection, and you protected me. It's my money, and I want you to have it. You did honest work, and it is an honest wage." With that she punctuated her statement with a bounce of her head.

"I made out the bill," confessed Kevin. "I know you wouldn't have wanted me to, but Knox did want me to. How could I say no to her?"

How indeed, said Nattie to herself. "I appreciate that, Knox, but you should keep this money. Now that Trace Noble has been convicted and sentenced to life, I'll be getting the WXBQ fifty-thousand-dollar reward."

Knox burrowed up under Kevin's arm. "You know," she said coyly, "we could go away somewhere and start working on your book."

"The First-Timers' Guide to Italy," wondered Kevin.

"I don't think we could go to Italy on thirty-five hundred dollars, but we could take a road trip and work on your Weird Products coffee-table book."

For years Kevin had collected pictures of oddities, especially odd or unique products. It started with unique flavors of M&M'S and progressed to items like pickle-flavored toothpaste and beer shampoo. Nattie was beyond being surprised when they told her that Knox also collected pictures of odd products. Her collection included potted possum and cookie butter. The idea that they were collaborating on a coffee-table book was a surprise.

Nattie could see Kevin's cheeks bulge out from his smile, even though she was only looking at the back of his head.

"Isn't she great?" observed Kevin as he grinned over his shoulder at Nattie.

Nattie was delighted for them as she watched their dance. They seemed so suited for each other. *All is well in the land of romance,* she repeated to herself, and then she wondered again where Nathan was.

THE END . . . NOT

Characters in *Why Knox?*

Debbie	Nattie's friend
Doug "Duke" Schneider	SWVa detective
Dr. Callahan**	Bristol eye doc
Dr. Minter**	Kingsport orthopedic surgeon
Duane	Debbie's husband
Ed Snodderly**	Performed at R&R with Brandon Story
Eli Anderson	15-year-old kid who loves to bake
Emily Garcia*	Bodyguard from Kingsport
Esther Dabney Kerr*	Social worker; Susan Renee's supervisor
Frank Lester	Was attacked in *Why Me?*
Gracie	Barmaid from Cherokee
Hiram Moreland	Nattie's mentor & Nathan's uncle
Ingrid O'Brien	Nattie's mother
Jack Taggert	Kingsport tavern owner
Jamie Cook	Black Lillies musician
Jana**	Barista from CityMug
Janine	Server from Stoney Knob
Jason	Cherokee PD sergeant
Jimmy	Nathan left him in charge of the Our House Tavern
Joanne Villars**	Owner of Black Snake Meadery
John Early	Bristol PD
Joyce**	Sam Samuel's wife
Karen*	Owner of George & Sid's
Kevin Johnson	Nattie's brother; office manager
Kim Lyons**	Sang at R&R with Annie Robinette
Knox DeVilla	Candy Farmer's stage name
Lauren Carrico Kinser*	Female vocalist from Dane & Taylor; also got the threatening note
Linda**	Server at Babycakes in Abingdon

Lionel O'Brien	Lawyer; Nattie's stepfather
Maggie Lawson**	2009 Miss Virginia Teen USA
Margarette Johns	RD at Livingston Academy
Marissa Ferguson	BPD detective and good friend to Nattie (from *Why Bristol?*)
Mark Andrews*	WXBQ DJ who got killed in the prologue
Mark Price**	Owner of Price's Kitchen
Mary Jane Blackstone	Susan Renee's last SW client
Mel Farmer	Knox's father
Nancy Sauls**	Co-owner of Sessions 27
Nathan Moreland	Nattie's ex-husband
Oddie Pruitt	Mary Jane's ex-boyfriend; sent to prison
Ollie Ruggiliano	Nattie's 1st client (from *Why Natasha?*)
Phyllis	Knox's grandmother
Red Molly	Band from NY
Roberta Farmer	Knox's mother
Robin Bailey**	Barista from the Grind House
Sam Bush**	Featured musician
Sam Samuel*	Bodyguard from Roanoke, VA
Samantha	Lionel's daughter from a previous marriage; Nattie's stepsister
Shelly Black	Nattie's best friend from HS
Sweeter	Masher from Silva
Skylar Lynch	Knox's ex-boyfriend; backup singer
Stacy Renee*	Susan Renee's sister
Steve Stroud*	WXBQ DJ who got killed in the prologue
Susan Renee	SW killed in the prologue
The Wolf	Nattie's grandfather
TomPrior*	Black Lillies musician
Trisha Gene Brady*	Female vocalist from Black Lillies; also got threatening note

For other titles, authors blog, photos,
and discount codes:

www.csthompsonbooks.com

Other titles in the WHY MYSTERY series:

Why Natasha?

Why Him?

Why Me?

Why Bristol?

www.ingramcontent.com/pod-product-compliance
Lightning Source LLC
Chambersburg PA
CBHW070559130626
46556CB00001B/214